RANDOM HOUSE
CHILDREN'S BOOKS

TITLE:	Hattie Mae Begins Again
AUTHOR:	Sharon G. Flake
IMPRINT:	Alfred A. Knopf BFYR
PUBLICATION DATE:	January 13, 2026
ISBN:	978-0-593-65034-9
TENTATIVE PRICE:	$17.99 US / $24.50 CAN
GLB ISBN:	978-0-593-65035-6
GLB TENTATIVE PRICE:	$20.99 US / $28.99 CAN
AUDIO ISBN (download):	979-8-217-17274-0
EBOOK ISBN:	978-0-593-65036-3
PAGES:	368
TRIM SIZE:	5-1/2" x 8-1/4"
AGES:	8–12

ATTENTION, READER: THESE ARE UNCORRECTED ADVANCE PROOFS FOR REVIEW PURPOSES. All trim sizes, page counts, months of publication, and prices should be considered tentative and subject to change without notice. Please check publication information and any quotations against the bound copy of the book. We urge this for the sake of editorial accuracy as well as for your legal protection and ours.

Please send any review or mention of this book to:
Random House Children's Books Publicity Department
rhkidspublicity@penguinrandomhouse.com

ALSO BY SHARON G. FLAKE

Bang!
Begging for Change
The Life I'm In
Money Hungry
Once in a Blue Moon
Pinned
The Skin I'm In
Unstoppable Octobia May

HATTIE MAE BEGINS AGAIN

SHARON G. FLAKE

ALFRED A. KNOPF NEW YORK

A Borzoi Book published by Alfred A. Knopf
An imprint of Random House Children's Books
A division of Penguin Random House LLC
1745 Broadway, New York, NY 10019
penguinrandomhouse.com
rhcbooks.com

Text copyright © 2026 by Sharon G. Flake
Jacket art copyright © 2026 by Brittney Bond

Penguin Random House values and supports copyright. Copyright fuels creativity, encourages diverse voices, promotes free speech, and creates a vibrant culture. Thank you for buying an authorized edition of this book and for complying with copyright laws by not reproducing, scanning, or distributing any part of it in any form without permission. You are supporting writers and allowing Penguin Random House to continue to publish books for every reader. Please note that no part of this book may be used or reproduced in any manner for the purpose of training artificial intelligence technologies or systems.

Knopf, Borzoi Books, and the colophon are registered trademarks of Penguin Random House LLC.

Editor: Gianna Lakenauth
Designer: Jade Rector
Production Editor: Melinda Ackell
Managing Editor: Jake Eldred
Production Manager: CJ Han

Library of Congress Cataloging-in-Publication Data is available upon request.
ISBN 978-0-593-65034-9 (trade) — ISBN 978-0-593-65035-6 (lib. bdg.) — ISBN 978-0-593-65036-3 (ebook)

The text of this book is set in 11.75 point Adobe Garamond Pro.

Manufactured in the United States of America
10 9 8 7 6 5 4 3 2 1

The authorized representative in the EU for product safety and compliance is Penguin Random House Ireland, Morrison Chambers, 32 Nassau Street, Dublin D02 YH68, Ireland, https://eu-contact.penguin.ie.

Random House Children's Books supports the First Amendment and celebrates the right to read.

To everyone who made their way to Philadelphia
during the Great Migration, thank you for your sacrifice,
determination, creativity, entrepreneurial spirit, and grit.
I shall forever be indebted to you, grateful,
for all you endured and accomplished.

HATTIE MAE BEGINS AGAIN

AUGUST 1938

STARTING OVER ON THE WRONG FOOT

MY NEW SCHOOL

Miss Abigail's School
 for Exceptional Young Ladies
is for well-to-do girls whose fathers are
lawyers, architects
 and engineers
politicians, surgeons
painters and doctors of note.

Ma is a plain old schoolteacher.
Daddy works on a factory floor.
 I do not belong here with these girls.

HIDING THE TRUTH FROM MY FAMILY

Since coming to school in Philadelphia
I write each week to my family.
A letter to Ma and Daddy
another for James Henry, my twin
and a short one to Gran.
    I fold them into threes
stick 'em into envelopes
    drop 'em off at Station D
a post office
    up the street.

I am having a grand time,
I tell everyone.
Miss Abigail's girls are loyal and kind.

But it isn't true.
Not a single word.

GRAN'S LAST WORDS

The night before I left for school
Gran asked me to meet her on the porch
    the one Granddad built extra wide
    'cause she asked him to.

I sat down beside Gran
who was rocking in her favorite chair.
She took my hand.

"When you get to Philadelphia
    do not shame the family.
Our good name
    is all we have."

"I understand, Gran."

She recounted
some of the things I'd done
that she wished I hadn't.
    Sassed grown folks.
Thrown coals at Titus, our old enemy.
Started an apple war against him and his kin.
Trained my birds to attack anyone
    who would not leave James Henry
alone to live his life in peace.

"I do not much care for the North,"
Gran told me.
"Our people running up there
like it's the promised land.
    But trouble be everywhere.
I'm sticking with the trouble I know."

I heard Negroes up North are different from us
more sophisticated than ones in Detroit
    where I was born
and in Seed County, North Carolina
where our family lived off and on for years.

Gran's eyes closed.
Mine too.
I imagined myself dressed to the nines
beautiful
in a green silk gown
and close-fitting gloves up to my elbows.

I thanked Gran for all she'd done for me
    especially for the new dresses
a crinoline slip
the pinafore she made herself
    a pair of two-dollar shoes besides.

She couldn't stop smiling.
    "Gotta keep up, you know.
Dress and behave the way you was raised.
Show them Northerners
    we ain't no country hicks down here.
We hardworking
God-fearing
make-a-way-out-of-no-way
    family people
who love the land like it was kin
tend to our own
    from the belly to the tomb."

I took ahold of a stone ring
dangling from my neck on twine.

A going-away present from Gran.
    "You got people, girl
no matter where you go or how far you stray.
Don't forget that up North.
    And remember . . ." she whispered.
"If you wanna come back home,
    come.
Ain't no harm in admitting
that something don't suit or fit you
the way you expected."

AN INVITATION TOO GOOD TO REFUSE

Miss Abigail is Ma's cousin.
A year ago she wrote us saying
I could attend her school if I wanted
    tuition-free.
I'd never heard of her before.

Cousin
did not want the other girls
to think she was playing favorites.
So me and her made a deal.
I was never to let on
    that we were related.
But some secrets can't be kept.
They're so big
they blow up in your face.

DADDY'S INSTRUCTIONS

Two days before I left for school
Daddy purchased me tickets for the Seaboard and the
Pennsylvania Railroad.
    He put me on the train on Wednesday with a kiss.
    Said to stay in the Colored section
even after I changed trains in Virginia.

"And for goodness' sake, Hattie Mae
do not be quarrelsome or talk about your rights.
Or wander off.
    We need you to arrive in Philadelphia alive
and in one piece."

MY GOOD-LUCK COAT

Daddy paid the woman beside me
one whole dollar
    to keep an eye on me.
I'm twelve.
Didn't need my hand held.
But Daddy wouldn't have it
any other way.

Before he left
he brought up the coat I was wearing
made of silky taffeta.
The same royal blue as the dress I had on.

I'd never owned anything so beautiful.

"Ain't it too warm to wear a coat in August?"
he wanted to know.

I was already sweating
down to my underwear.
    So, I laid the coat
over my lap careful-like
kept track of it the whole trip.

"In Philadelphia
    you have to look like somebody,"
my good friend Lottie Jean said before I left.
"Not a newcomer
or country bumpkin straight off the turnip truck."
She was born and raised in New York City
so she knows a thing or two.

10

It was her outfit I had on.
"For good luck,"
    she said, handing it over
with as much pride as Gran
when she handed me the ring.

GOODBYE FOR NOW, SEED COUNTY

The train jerked
pulled off with a start.
I watched Daddy through the window
running to keep up
waving until we both disappeared.
I cried.
The lady beside me
    reached over
        hugged me for miles.

COW GIRL

Before I knew it
we were passing farms
tobacco fields
cornstalks nearly ready for harvest
    cows resting on steep green hills.
        I mooed.
The lady beside me frowned.
    Said it was not good etiquette
to behave like a farm animal.
"Folks up North
    look down their noses at such behavior.
Leave it behind on the train. Please."

I told her I would.

CITY DREAMS

    I rested my eyes
pretended I was a different girl.
Not Brother's twin
nor Ma's only daughter
nor Gran's favorite.
    I was a girl of means
a daughter of high society.
Well-dressed
like the girls at boarding school surely would be.
Fancy
as women and girls
in the Negro newspapers
Uncle sneaked off the train
    when he was a Pullman porter.

He'd hide the newspaper
inside the one meant for whites.
    Carry it off the train
rolled and tucked underneath his arm
till it was safe to pass along
to Negroes in our neck of the woods
    eager to know if the stories from up North were true:
good wages aplenty
equality
ten jobs to every man and woman
indoor plumbing
freedom to live and dream big as you pleased
equality.

CROSSING OVER

A girl about my age
cheered
soon as the train
crossed the Mason-Dixon Line.
Her little brother frowned
stood up and shouted,
"I don't see no line."
Their mother said it couldn't be seen,
    like chalk on the ground
with the naked eye.

"But it's there all right . . ."
She reached for his hands.
    "And I'm mighty glad
to be on this side of it."

THE END OF THE LINE

The lady Daddy paid to watch over me
handed my luggage to a porter
who aided me down the train steps.

On the platform
I got swallowed up by strangers
passengers with fast-moving feet
some carrying luggage held together
with belts better suited for trousers
    others toting their belongings
    in fifty-pound feed sacks
hoisted over their shoulders.

I thought about what Gran told me.
"The North be calling our folk
like a siren at sea."

Wide-eyed
all of us looked here and there
for a familiar face
hopeful.

WELCOME TO PHILADELPHIA

"Look for Cousin," Daddy told me.
"Her hair is fire-engine red."

Cousin was nowhere to be found.
But outside I did see my name
    written on white cardboard
spelled out in cursive
like I was important.
    Hattie Mae Jenkins

A man
tall and brown as Uncle
held the sign high over his head.
Proud-like.

He was dressed smartly
in a navy blue uniform
    with six gold buttons on the jacket.
"Welcome, Hattie Mae.
I'm Mr. Gage."
    He tipped the black cap on his head.

I curtsied.
Felt like a queen.

"You are very fortunate, young lady.
Philadelphia is the greatest city on earth."
He bowed.
"Once you have been here awhile
    you will forget the *South*
and her *country* ways ever existed."

RIDING IN STYLE

Mr. Gage went up to a black Cadillac
freshly washed and waxed.
Seemed like it could hold the moon
it was so big inside.

He put my suitcase in the trunk.
Opened the back door.
Bowed again.
    Helped me inside.

The thick leather seats
felt smooth as butter.
    Not that I could enjoy 'em.
I did not want my hair
pressed and curled with Vaseline
    to ruin his seats.
So I sat stiff and straight
    and kept my mouth shut.

LITTLE GIRL IN THE BIG CITY

Philadelphia is fast and loud.
Downtown
cars beeped and sped up the street.
Buses and trolleys seemed angry as people.
    Negroes and whites hurried past each other
fanning the heat away with hats and handkerchiefs
bare hands and church fans.

At a red light a little girl waved.
Made me feel welcome.
    I waved back.
Gave her a big old Seed County smile.

A woman
    in a hurry
tore up the street.
She was dressed in a pin-striped pantsuit
and a pillbox hat that leaned sideways.
She looked important.
I want to be important someday.

Men wore suits
and white shirts with gold cuffs,
    creased pants
with the wrinkles ironed out.
Some in work uniforms—
checkered shirts
and dungarees and thick dirty boots—
    reminded me of Daddy.

Mr. Gage pointed out the window.

"Them smokestacks over yonder is where some of the men are coming from. Factories all over Philadelphia, you know."

SAME BUT DIFFERENT

From Chestnut Street to Market to Broad
my eyes went from one tall building to the next.
One department store to another.
Gimbels
    Wanamaker's
Lit Brothers.
    I wondered if they had a five-and-dime store
Woolworth's. If the stores here let you try on clothes inside.
We couldn't in Seed County.
Not *us* anyhow.

Sitting back, forgetting myself
I watched Negroes and whites
board buses and trolleys at the same stop.
Get on in whatever order they liked.

A woman Ma's skin color tried to hail a cab
but kept getting passed up.
Gran and us know about such things.

MEETING MOTHER BETHEL

Mr. Gage drove to South Philadelphia
    the Seventh Ward. Told me about Engine 11,
a fire station. Said there was a school close by for Colored youth.
He said he would give me a history lesson on them
    some other time.

"For now, follow me," he said, opening the door.
"And let me say this:
They ain't better over there on Christian Street
where you'll be.
    Just better off."

We didn't go far, just across the street.
    "It's time you met Mother."

"Your mother? Where is she?"
I looked around.

He laughed. "No. Not mine."
    Mr. Gage walked up to the church
parked himself on the steps
but not before he pulled out a handkerchief to sit on.
    "This is Mother Bethel AME Church.
More than souls get saved here."

I tiptoed up to the door and stared inside.
Eyed stained glass windows
that told stories about the history of the church
and God's role in it.
There were wooden benches to sit and pray on downstairs
and a balcony-full upstairs.
The pulpit, grand and shiny, had organ pipes behind it.

The founder, Richard Allen
is entombed in another part of the church, Mr. Gage told me.

"The room is all white, marble, a fitting tribute to a man who accomplished so much for so many.
May we never forget his name."

BETTING ON US

I sat down next to Mr. Gage
who talked about himself this time.

How he came to Philadelphia, barefooted and empty-handed.
    No coat to block the cold and wind, he told me
no place to lay his head come nightfall.
No family or job waiting for him once he got here.

"It wasn't just me. No, sir.
Lots of us arrived that way
    hundreds a day
thousands most likely.
Hungry
tired
our pockets light as feathers.
But we rolled up our shirtsleeves nonetheless
worked any job we could get
determined to make a better life for ourselves
and our families.
One painted by us this time
    and nobody else.

CROSSING BRIDGES

"Mother and other churches
saw to it we got tended to
fed and looked after like they birthed us.
Still do."

"Mother Bethel . . . she helped you?"

"Ten years ago
I spent my last dime on a train ride from Alabama.
Ended up in Jersey picking peaches and apples
    making pennies on a dollar.
Three years later
broke and bone-tired
I walked across the Delaware River Bridge
into Philadelphia.
Never looked back."

Another handkerchief came out his back pocket.
How many he got? I thought.
    He patted his forehead dry.
"All I needed was a chance
a suit—new or used.
One piping hot meal
a pair of size-eleven boots.
I'd do the rest, I told an usher at Mother Bethel.
The next week I had this job too."
    Now he's the chauffeur, he told me
the maintenance man,
whatever Cousin Abigail wants him to be.

Mr. Gage stared up at the building.
Said Mother Bethel was his North Star.

"Who would I be without her?"

CHRISTIAN STREET: DOCTOR'S ROW

Back in the car
I poked my head out the window
watched houses go by
    rows and rows of 'em
close as books on a library shelf.
Red brick.
    Marble steps.
Single doors and doubles.
Three-story houses, mostly.
My favorites
had windows curved at the top
like eyebrows.

Pulling onto Christian Street
Mr. Gage said lots of doctors lived on this block.

"Do you have to be a doctor to live here?" I asked him.

"No, indeed.
There're all sorts of people here.
    Janitors, stevedores, hairdressers.
Elites and high-society folk
who show up in the newspaper
in ball gowns, hosting charity events
glad-handing Mayor Wilson
giving him an earful sometimes too
about poor-quality housing
juvenile crime on the rise and other conditions that
    need attention in the city.
    "I could live on this street if I wanted.
But the Seventh Ward suits me like a glove."

FINALLY, COUSIN'S SCHOOL

Five stories high.
Seventeen windows on just the front.
Cousin Abigail's school
sat on the corner, showing off.
Excited
I jumped out the car
ran up the steps.

Mr. Gage said nicely,
"The door, young lady.
You forgot to close it.
    And what about your purse?"

Back I went
crossing the sidewalk
where I almost got run down by a boy on a bike.

MR. GAGE AND THE BOY WITH POOR MANNERS

Mr. Gage pulled me back just in the nick of time.
He blamed the boy for the error
    like I had no fault in it.
    "Where's your manners, boy?" he asked him.
    "Sorry." He lifted up a brown paper bag.
"I have a delivery to make. Shoes just repaired."

"Well . . . be more careful next time."
    "Yes, sir."

He reminded me of Brother, that boy.
He seemed small for his age
had kind eyes and an easy smile.
    "I'm Alabaster." He looked my way.
"What's your name?"

"Hattie Mae."

"You're the new girl.
The newspaper said you were coming.
    Welcome, Miss Hattie."

"Newspaper?"
I looked up at Mr. Gage.
    He reached in his pants pocket
took out a nickel
    flipped it Alabaster's way.
"Run along, boy."

"See you soon." And just like that
Alabaster was gone.

CHOOSING WHICH ROAD TO TAKE

Watching Alabaster ride off
Mr. Gage issued me a warning.
    "Philadelphia is made up
of all sorts.
"Everybody ain't Marian Anderson
or Du Bois, you know.
Some just plain rude
and money can't buy manners.
Others don't have a dime
and got kings and queens inside 'em.
    Choose for yourself
        the road you want to take
            the person you want to be."

THE TRUTH ABOUT COUSIN'S SCHOOL

Cousin
used to board girls from every part of the country.
Then the Depression hit.
    It emptied beds and desks
took the school from eighty girls to twenty-two
to fourteen.

Not that she ever told me.
The girls here talk a lot.

WHAT I SAW AT COUSIN'S SCHOOL

        It was nearly too much for me
Cousin's school
like stepping into a fancy magazine
    a fine painting
a museum.

My eyes couldn't stay put
there were so many things to see:
    ceilings tall as cypress trees
halls wide as Gran's whole house
    satin wallpaper
        soft as flowers in a garden
velvet couches in ruby red and midnight blue
crystal chandeliers everywhere
    one in the foyer to greet you.
Three in the hall between the foyer and the kitchen.

I pinched myself,
wondered if I was dreaming.

THE GIRLS WHO ATTEND
MISS ABIGAIL'S SCHOOL

Mr. Gage left me in the foyer
went to tell Cousin I was here.
Soon as he disappeared
the front door flew open and fourteen girls
dressed to the nines
    quiet as feathers
walked in the house.
Ignoring me
they took the stairs
    two at a time
carrying instruments of one kind or another.

Everything about them was different.
Their hair was curled in ringlets
down to their shoulders.
    They'd probably die before using rag ties
at night like me.

Their skin looked soft and shiny.
    From time to time
we used bacon grease to keep ash and dryness away.
Those girls used something store-bought
I could tell.

One of them had on perfume
that swallowed up the whole room.
Turned it into a flower garden.
Roses and lavender.

A girl with light brown hair

stopped at the top of the steps
stared down at me long and hard.
   She did not think much of me
I could tell.
Turns out I was right.

A QUICK TRIP HOME

I wandered the halls
made my way to the parlor.
Admired myself in the mirror over the mantel
above the fireplace.

I wasn't dressed like the other girls
but I'd do, I told myself.
And for good measure
I took out a comb
ran it through my hair.
Then it happened.
I was home again, wrangling chickens
milking cows
but I did not let my mind stay there.

A KIND AND CHEERFUL GIRL

One of Cousin Abigail's girls walked in
carrying a silver tray
apologizing for Cousin's delay.
She was dressed in her Sunday best
    like the others on the stairs
wearing a brooch on her blouse
shaped like a Scottie dog.

"My name is Bert. Welcome.
Miss Abigail will be along shortly."
    "I'm Hattie Mae."

"You must be famished."

I was.
The chicken, boiled eggs and buttered cornbread
packed by Gran
were long gone
eaten a little at a time
on the train, every four hours
as instructed.

Bert set the tray on a green velvet ottoman.
Handed me a cup of hot tea on a saucer
    along with a warm biscuit smeared with plum jelly.

"Sugar? Honey?"

"Sugar, thank you."
I took more than I should have.
Six cubes. But Bert didn't seem to mind.

SWEATING MY HAIR OUT

Bert filled my cup.
Plopped down on the coach
and told me they had just returned
from giving a recital.
"Which instrument do you play?" she asked.

None. But I thought it best
to keep that to myself.
      "The violin," I said confidently.

She smiled. Said she played the violin as well.
"But I am new to it. Perhaps you could give me some pointers.
The oboe and clarinet are more my speed."

I nearly choked on my tea.

"The recital was for newcomers to our city.
It was held at a recreation center
the Catharine Street YWCA.
We welcomed the newcomers with
      a classical piece
calm and pleasing
written by Miss Abigail herself.
Volunteers fed the visitors until they were full
then provided them with information
about settlement houses
the Salvation Army
and other places they could find a bed for free or a room to rent
      at affordable prices.

Changing subjects, Bert asked
if I wished to relieve myself of my coat.

I did
but said I was fine enough.

"In Philadelphia
we do our best not to wear coats indoors
especially when it's eighty-six degrees out," she told me.

Sweat jumped off my forehead
swam in my tea.
But I left my coat on.

MAKING THE NEWS

Bert reached into her shirt pocket
and pulled out a newspaper article
folded in squares. She kindly passed it on to me.

    I set my cup down.
Smiled from the first line to the last.

Miss Hattie Mae Jenkins
12 years old
Route 28
Seed County, North Carolina
is the latest student at the prestigious
Miss Abigail's School for Exceptional Young Ladies.
Her mother, Alberta, is an educator.
Her father, George, is a factory worker.
Headmistress Abigail Gooden assures us
young Hattie won't have any trouble keeping pace
with her contemporaries.

We are certain Hattie Mae
will be a bright light to our people
and do Philadelphia and the school extremely proud.
    Good luck, Hattie Mae.
    We are counting on you.

MURDER

"The *Philadelphia Tribune* said this about me?"
I read the article again.

"Yes, it was on the Society page."

"Just today
a boy I met told me I was in the newspaper."

Bert asked his name.

"Ala . . . baster?"

"Oh, we all know him.
    One of the girls calls him
the school's pet."

It was hard to hold my tongue
knowing how much Alabaster reminded me of Brother.
    "Being rich does not give people
the right to be ill-mannered," I told Bert.

"Some girls here believe their families' standing in society
    gives them a pass to do as they like," Bert said.
"Especially Lisa. You'll meet her.
Her father
contributes a great deal to the school.
    So, she gets away with murder."

WHAT BERT TOLD ME ABOUT LISA

Bert crossed her legs when I did.
Scratched her cheek like me too.
But she was bright and cheery
so I didn't mind so much.

"We learn a great deal at this institution," she told me,
    "and get along exceptionally well with each other.
The majority of us do anyhow."

She leaned in closer.
Told me to be cautious of that girl Lisa.
    "She is a bitter pill to swallow.
Not always awful, but when she is
    she is awfully horrible," Bert whispered.
"She puts on airs.
But there are those who follow her regardless.
Like Dorothy and Ethel, who we call Eiffel Tower
because of her height."

I set my cup and saucer on my lap.
Thought about Titus from Seed County.
He was awful for a long time but improved,
I told Bert.

Being hopeful
I said maybe Lisa would too.

Right then she walked in.
It was the girl on the steps with the light brown hair.
Two other girls trailed behind her.

Bert held my hand.

"She will not make you feel good about your coat.
Please
let me help you out of it."

This time I listened.

THE MEANEST GIRL IN THE WORLD

Lisa sniffed
    the way Gran would
after me and Brother had a long day
of fun in the sun and the woods.
    She pinched her nose closed.
"Did I hear Miss Abigail say you were from South Carolina?"

Before I could answer
she turned her nose loose
    but kept a frown on her face.
"Alabama?
    Georgia?
You must come from one of those states.
Those people always find themselves up here."

Her two friends laughed.
I reached for my necklace
held on tight
wishing Brother was here.

RIFFRAFF LIKE ME

Stirring her tea
    Lisa asked me to lift my foot.

"Pardon?" I said
trying to behave like a girl with class.

"I would like to check your heels.
For dirt."

I looked at Bert.
    Lisa blew on her tea.
Took a sip.
"Once
I was introduced to a girl with red clay on the soles of her boots.
She was from Georgia, it turned out.
I suspected as much all along."

"Does it matter?"
    Bert asked.

I patted my foot.
Bit my lip to hold my peace.

Bert set my cup and saucer on the silver tray.

Lisa kept at it.
    "Philadelphia is filling up with riffraff of one kind or
    another.
    If it persists, Father says
we shall have to leave posthaste."

I was the riffraff she was talking about.

Me.
Hattie Mae in my two-dollar shoes
and borrowed dress.

Gran wouldn't mind, I was sure
if I socked Lisa in the mouth.
But I thought better of it.
Held my hands behind my back
    willed 'em not to turn into fists.

A FAMILY TO BE PROUD OF

Bert got Lisa to change directions
by asking her to tell me about her father.
He's a surgeon
    a professor too.
Lisa couldn't stop talking about him.
    "He teaches young men
at Morehouse College in Atlanta to be physicians.
He is a very important person, soon to be president
at one of the hospitals in the city."

Bert crossed her legs when the other girls did.
Asked if it was Frederick Douglass Memorial Hospital
Lisa was speaking of.

Lisa ignored the question.
    Said she receives a letter from her parents
twice a week.
Lots of presents too
like a fur coat shipped from Italy.
Perfume from France.
A lovely silk scarf from Mexico.

Bert folded her arms when Lisa did.
Cut her eyes my way.
Whispered,
"He hasn't written her since April or May.
And the presents stopped coming
a long time ago."

And what about her mother? I asked.
Bert answered.
"Oh, she passed.

But her stepmother is a writer
living and teaching in France.
    Home twice a year, I hear."

DIGGING UP RELATIVES

I swallowed
and thought about my family.
Ma
the best teacher in the world.
And Uncle
who used to be a Pullman porter.

I dug around in my brain for other relatives.
Did not find one doctor, lawyer or writer
in the whole bunch
but still
plenty of people to be proud of nonetheless
    Gran would say.

NOTHING BUT THE TRUTH

I
told Lisa we had sharecroppers in our family.
"Slaves too once
along with nursemaids
folks who crossed the plains
    by wagon train, so Gran says.
Woodworkers and ironworkers
bricklayers
Freemasons
quilters.
My aunt Bess was a solider for the Union army.
They never knew she was a girl."

I did not mention Cousin Abigail's father
Uncle Robert
who fought in France during World War I
the 93rd Infantry Division
and never went back to the South.
He made his way to Philadelphia
found a way to be Colored and rich.
Didn't reach out to the family again.
Gran thought he was dead.
After he passed
it was Cousin who extended her hand.

I stood up proud.
"My family owns land in North Carolina.
Granddad built a house on it.
Taught himself to read and write.
Paid Ma's way to Wilberforce outright."

Don't say anything more,

I could hear James Henry say
but I had to.
    "Gran is the best laundress
in Seed County.
No one can get clothes as white or wrinkle-free."

Lisa went too far when she said,
    "Well, perhaps Miss Abigail should hire her.
One can never have too many maids, you know."

I shoved her good and hard.
    I had to.
Not that I meant for her to fall on her keister.

CONSEQUENCES FOR MY BEHAVIOR

No one told me to. I just did it—
carried myself and my things into Cousin's office
and told on myself.

I took a seat across from her desk
waited for her to ship me home, no postage due.
Only she didn't.

Her arms were crossed.

"There are important girls
from important families attending my school.
Some from the oldest families in Philadelphia. O.P.'s
Old Philadelphia, we call them. Lisa is from such a family.
    Bert also, though her temperament is more soothing."
Cousin whispered like there were ears listening
on the other side of the door.
    "Word cannot get out
that one of my girls is having difficulty governing her behavior.
Is that understood?"

"Yes . . . Cousin."

"We are not related, remember?"
She winked. I shook my head yes.
Stared down at my hands
folded tight as crab claws.

"It's just how it has to be." Her voice was kind and steady.
Standing
Cousin Abigail said I was to meet her in the dining room
tomorrow at sunrise.

Wasn't the moon still out then?

Nonetheless my eyes met hers. "Yes . . . Miss Abigail."

"You are not being punished, understood?"

Whenever grown-ups say that
    most likely you are.

INDOOR PLUMBING

After my meeting with Cousin
Bert showed up and took my suitcase.
Escorting me upstairs, she told me not to worry.
"Miss Abigail really is very fair.
    She lost another student last week.
I think it worries her."

In the middle of the hall
    I spotted the bathroom
and stopped in my tracks.
Leaving Bert, I walked inside
stared at the stalls
ten in a row
along with six squeaky-clean sinks
and white tile floors with black diamonds etched in 'em.
    In Seed County
we did our business outside in tall, skinny shacks
that looked like closets with doors
with holes in the ground
    for standing or squatting over.
Those
were our toilets.
    Outhouses to be exact.

BERT, MY NEW ROOMMATE

On our bedroom door
there was a sign.
    Welcome, Hattie Mae

And a drawing of two girls holding hands
with the sun up high
and butterflies all around 'em.

"Thank you, Bert."

She stepped aside
    let me go in first.
"The bed by the window is for you.
    It was mine
but I wanted you to feel special."

I did
just by having her here, I told her.
But inside I was ashamed of myself
    for breaking my promise to Gran.

SECOND THOUGHTS ABOUT COUSIN'S SCHOOL

Back home
I shared a bed with Brother
and we shared a room with Gran.

But here
Bert and me each have a desk
a vanity
and a closet, each with crystal doorknobs.

No two rooms are alike, Bert told me.
     "Miss Abigail made sure of it."

The walls in our room are pink
light as frosting on a birthday cake.

The hardwood floor, shiny like glass
has an expensive-looking throw rug in the middle.

A set of white linen curtains hangs at each window
tied back with giant white bows.

The wall over Bert's desk has posters
with movie stars on them
men and women
Negro and white
     crooners and musicians alike.

It's the kind of room girls dream about.
But if I could have gone home
right then and there
I would have.

TITLE TK

I went over to the window.
Told Bert about brother and me stargazing
pretending we were space explorers
taking off in a rocket ship from Gran's rooftop.

She stood beside me.
    Did not comment on my tears.

What if I never fit in? I said.
And none of the girls accept me?
Or I get sent home
a disappointment to my family.

Bert put her arm over my shoulder.
Said most girls find their way here eventually.
"And you will too."

PROOF

That night
quiet as snow
    I tiptoed over to the closet
hoping not to wake Bert.
Sitting down, I grabbed my shoe
and found the proof Lisa was searching for.
Dirt on the soles
carried here from North Carolina
    along with all my other belongings.

Before I left home
I took a walk in Gran's garden.
Squatted
talked to her tomatoes
said goodbye to okra long as Daddy's fingers
and cabbages wide as my belly.

Careful as a spider
    just as quick
I shoved those shoes into my suitcase
zipped it up lickety-split.
Pushed it to the back of my closet
along with my country ways and tone.
Then crawled into bed
holding tight to Gran's necklace.

HIGH SOCIETY

I'd never tell Ma or Gran.
Not even Brother.
But I've always wanted to end up on the Society page.
To be important
do something worth writing about.
Lead the sorts of social clubs the newspapers report on.
Get married to an upstanding citizen.
Have my picture taken at tea parties
and brunches
charity affairs and candlelit dinners
raise funds for the less fortunate.

A top-rate education
is the quickest route to that sort of life, I believe.

COUSIN AND ME ALONE TOGETHER

When Cousin and I got to the dining room
it was still dark out.
I yawned a lot.
    Tried to hide it.

Mrs. Dreamer, our cook
was in the kitchen
frying bacon
stirring something in a pot
singing one of Mahalia Jackson's tunes.

Cousin Abigail walked across the room
opening china cabinets filled with dishes for every occasion.
Christmas
the Fourth of July
Thanksgiving.
Birthdays.
There were turkey platters
plates with the American flag on 'em
    ones with trees covered in snow.
Ones for spring
bright yellow
with pink tulips around the edges.
She pointed.
    "We'll need eighteen of everything
sets of silverware included . . ."

A PERFECT TEAM

I set place mats on the tables
and plates on the mats.
Opened drawers
took out silverware
    sixty-seven pieces in all.

Cousin looked like she felt sorry for me.
"Usually
a team of girls is responsible for
setting the tables."
Her hands went out.
"Would you like to do it together?"

We folded cloth napkins side by side.
    Put coasters under drinking glasses.
    Set platters in the center for
        the bacon and sausage links
    put out bowls for oatmeal
fresh fruit and cottage cheese
one dish for biscuits and another for gravy.

A hour later
we were still at it
with Cousin shifting forks and butter knives I misplaced
deciding that cracked or dull plates
would never do for her girls.

She stretched her back.
    Asked if I was tired
hurting from all the bending
and lifting.

I lived on a farm a lot of my life.
Chased runaway pigs.
Emptied the outhouse bucket
plenty of times.
Helped make apples into jelly and jam.
    "I'm not tired yet," I said.

FIRST

Sweat
was crawling down the back of my neck
by the time Cousin dismissed me.
I was to go upstairs and wash quickly.
Put on my uniform
join the other girls at the top of the stairs.

"We line up alphabetically," Cousin Abigail told me.
"With our heads held high and mouths sealed
we head downstairs in an orderly fashion
    to partake of a good, hearty breakfast."
Discipline.
    Order.
A keen, inquisitive mind
and full stomach
helps one enter the day prepared,
Cousin said.

In a flash
    I was dressed
        the first in line.

THE DAY I PRETENDED TO BE A PRINCESS

I wanted to skip down the spiral staircase
or tap-dance the whole way
like Shirley Temple in the movies.
    Nobody back home would mind if I did.
But here we wear uniforms.
Plaid skirts.
Burgundy jackets with a lion's head crest on the left
    white shirts with too many buttons.
And we are expected to behave like young ladies
worthy of our station in life.

On my way down
I held my head high
    like there was a crown on it.
Pretended I was a princess
a queen.
Brother and Lottie Jean would have understood.

WHAT THE GIRLS SAID ABOUT ME AT THE TABLE

Bert sat next to me at breakfast.
I was all smiles.
Listening mostly
with my elbows on the table
not that I noticed.
It was Lisa who brought it to my attention.
She mentioned it to one girl
who whispered it to another
until nearly everyone at our table
was smirking and talking about me.
    Not Bert, of course.

I snapped to attention.
    "Back home it's no problem.
Ma doesn't believe in putting on airs."
    "See. I told you," Lisa said.
"Her kind does not belong here."

ALL EYES ON ME

Cousin changed the conversation.
Asked me
to share a little bit
    about myself.
My hopes and dreams too.

I wiped my lips
    set my napkin in my lap.
Kept my arms under the table.
"One day I might be a judge."
    "There are no Negro judges
in Philadelphia," Lisa said, shaking her head.
"And surely you will not be the first."

"Maybe a lawyer, then.
Or a baby doctor. I've been mulling things over."

I'm not sure what I said
to make Eiffel Tower laugh hard enough
that food shot out her mouth, but it did.
Another girl chuckled.
But two other girls stood up for me
saying high standards aren't just for men and boys.
Girls and women can also change the world.
Cousin agreed.

Lisa raised her hand.
"I believe a woman's place is in the home
cheering on her husband's accomplishments.
    Rearing children who will benefit society."
She claimed to want seven children.
"It's a good, solid number, I think."

Marigold lifted her arm next
    and got called on by Cousin.
"I plan to be a scientist
    a biologist, to be exact.
There are diseases our people have
that do not get properly addressed.
    I wish to remedy that."

I felt proud of myself.
    More girls joined in.
Sharon, an equestrian
wants to own a horse farm
to teach children to ride and compete.
Another girl plans to own a chain of hospitals across the South.
Nancy will be founder and president of her own college, she
told us.
    "And follow in the footsteps of Mary McLeod Bethune.
To fight for the rights of girls."

Cousin looked proud as a peacock.
At the end of our meal
    she dismissed us with a smile.
I was nearly out the room when Lisa found me.

"A wife and mother are as important
as any other job."

"Ma says so," I told Lisa.

She stared at my necklace.
    "What is *that* made from?"

I almost didn't say.
"Granite."

Someone threw a piece at Great-Gran
when she was a child.
It left her blind in one eye.
Her father made them pay.
　　　Gran wasn't sure how exactly.
Just that our family ended up with two hundred dollars
along with two cows, which they sold soon after.
That money was used to move them out of town
to purchase land
build a house
　　　and settle down.

Good can come out of bad,
her father told her. "The ring was proof of that,"
Gran said when she passed it on to me.

DRESSING UP FOR DINNER

Cousin tapped on my door.
Let herself in.
"At dinner girls are required to dress polished and smart.
    Do you have something appropriate to wear?"

"Yes, ma'am."
I was grinning from ear to ear. "I enjoy dressing up."

I wore one of Lottie Jean's outfits.
    It was fuchsia
had a red ribbon for a belt
and a stylish silk beret for my head.

I could practically hear Gran say,
If there's a prettier girl in this world
    I never met her.

STILL HERE

I was at school two whole weeks
before I set eyes on
    the mailman.
He stood on the sidewalk
waving a handful of letters.
I rushed off the porch to get 'em.
On my way into the house
    I set the other mail down.
Took what was mine.

Brother sent me a postcard.
Said all was well and I was missed.
For me to check the moon tonight
and think of him.

I threw back the blankets
stepped into slippers an inch too big.
Crossed the room.
Opened the curtains.
Smiled up at the moon and waved.
"How you doing, Brother?
Me, myself, I'm good. Missing you, though.
It's been fourteen days since I left Seed County.
Can you believe it?
    Seems like lots more."

WHAT BERT'S ROAMING EYES SAW

As soon as we got to class
Cousin handed us a surprise quiz.
    I went to work right away.

Bert
tried to get my attention.
    "My answer to question sixteen is ten.
Is that correct?"
    "Yes. Now, quiet."

A little while later she was at it again.
This time Cousin stomped her way over to us.
"Alberta McNeilly, keep your eyes on your own paper
    or I'll put horse blinders on you."

"I would never cheat!" Bert looked my way.
Folded her arms like she was cross.

I stuck up for her 'cause she's my one true friend here.
"She wasn't cheating." I lifted my right hand. "I swear."
    Though her eyes stayed glued to my paper a great deal.

Bert said she was only double-checking
to see if she had the right answers.

"Did you?" Cousin Abigail asked
with doubt in her eyes.

Bert smiled from ear to ear.
    "Every single one."

Then she ought to trust herself more,
Cousin told her.

LEFT BEHIND

Bert isn't as popular
as the other girls.
But they like her well enough.
Me
I take a bit of getting used to
some in Seed County think.

After lunch
we were to take our daily constitutional
a stroll
calisthenics in the basement
or some other such exercise.

The teachers were all in a meeting
discussing wages.
They hadn't had a raise in three years,
Bert told me.
Then she took off without me.

So did the other girls.
Arm in arm they left the block
speaking of boys they were fond of
losing weight
exchanging jewelry later that night.

I was alone on the porch
    when he showed up.

ALABASTER TO THE RESCUE

He smiled.
    Me too.
He waved.
    So did I.

Soon enough he rode his bike over to the steps
and introduced himself
again.
"I'm Alabaster."

"I remember you.
    We met before."

"Well
you sure are pretty, Miss Hattie."

I asked why he called me "Miss."
His mom makes him call all
Miss Abigail's girls that, he said,
"Smart as y'all are."

GOOD COMPANY ON A NICE FALL DAY

Dressed in a tweed cap
wearing bib overalls
Alabaster reminded me of the South:
    of fresh-washed clothes drying on the line outdoors
farms with bales of hay out front
hogs fattened for slaughter
Sunday supper with a table full of family
dirt roads to run up
kindness overflowing
home.

He hopped off his bike
sat on the steps beside me.
Together we watched girls across the street
    take turns jumping double Dutch.

"Wish I knew how to do that,"
I said.

He'd teach me one day, he told me.
    "Just as soon as I teach myself."

I laughed
and laughed
and laughed
until I remembered
it was nearly time for class again.

KEEPING UP WITH MY ASSIGNMENTS

Once school was over
    I ran to my room
pulled out my books
started studying
and studying
    sharpening pencils in between
answering questions
    solving math and science problems
    researching definitions of words
writing an essay afterward about William Penn
    the city's founder
stuck on top of city hall forever.

BERT'S DOUBLE

At supper
without being told
before a single girl showed up to eat
I set the entire table all by myself.
     Folded the napkins into triangles
like I was taught.
Used a crystal pitcher
heavy as a small dog
and filled every glass nearly full
some with ice and cold water
     others with apple juice or ginger ale.

A few girls
applauded me on their way in.

"See, give them time," Bert said.
     "They'll come around."

I took a seat across from her
watched her eat spoonfuls of pepper pot stew
chew and swallow without slurping
pat her lips properly.
     This time I copied her.

ALL BY MYSELF AGAIN

Once we're done with lunch and chores on Saturdays
we can do as we please
    for a little while anyhow.

Bert left again
without saying where she was off to.
She is prone to disappearing
I noticed.

Lisa and her friends
found a movie to attend.
Eiffel Tower made sure to let me know
    I was in no way invited.

The other girls went this way and that
to a teahouse in Delaware
the free library downtown and the roller-skating rink.
I went to my room. At my desk
hunched over a composition book
I studied Latin until my eyes hurt.
Ben, bene, bon
are root words meaning "good" or "well."
Using a dictionary
I found words derived from them.
Wrote 'em down in cursive.
    Repeated them out loud.

"Beneficial.
Bon voyage." The French say that for goodbye.
It's a noun.

"Benefit, benevolent, benign."

They all mean something different.
But good is at the root of 'em.
　　It binds them together
like blood binds kin.

I was finished
ready for bed, when Bert walked in.
　　"Hush," she said,
sliding into bed fully dressed.
A minute later Cousin Abigail showed up.
　　Made sure we were both present. "Lights out," she said.

MY BROTHER'S KEEPER

Second period
on the way to Mrs. Grable's class
I tried to get Bert to tell me where she went last night.
She wouldn't. We ended up laughing about Alabaster.
    She is certain he likes me.

I was barely in my seat when Mrs. Grable brought up
volunteering
    in our own community.

That got me to thinking about Seed County.
The way we looked out for each other.
    Clearing a neighbor's land after a storm.
Carting chicken soup to somebody's home
when sickness showed up.
Picking grasshoppers off crops
    by the bucketful.

I put my hand up.
    "I'd like to volunteer."

WHAT WE TALKED ABOUT IN CLASS

Sitting on the front row
Lisa patted her curls.
"It is high time our people learned to do for themselves.
Father says so and I agree."

People in this community
have a long history of lending a hand
and lifting others up, Mrs. Grable told us.
"Who would agree?"

Ten hands went up high. Mrs. Grable smiled
walked over to the board. Wrote down a list of places
we could volunteer next spring. Bert asked why
we couldn't choose for ourselves.
    Mrs. Grable told us she wasn't opposed to it.

Lisa said she would write her father about it.
    "He never forces me to do anything against my will."

I leaned left.
    "What about you, Bert?"

"I already volunteer."
    "Where?" I asked. The movie theater, I nearly said.
        She ignored me.

WORKING TO IMPROVE MYSELF

My penmanship isn't like the other girls'.
Even Mrs. Grable noticed.
    It can be hard to read.
The letters slant
and run too close together.

Ma taught me better.
Her handwriting is elegant
filled with loops and smooth lines.
I take after Daddy.
    It's hard to tell my *e*'s from my *c*'s
my *h*'s from my *b*'s sometimes.
    I never minded until now.
It got the job done.

Alone in the library after class
I dipped my fountain pen in the well
    practiced writing until my fingers cramped.
"That-a-girl, Hattie Mae," I heard Ma's voice say.

HOW WE DO THINGS DOWN SOUTH

Done practicing
I started drawing cone flowers from Gran's garden
the rusty weather vane on top of Mr. Nicole's barn
    along with rainbows in the sky.

Lisa walked in
    sat down across from me.
"Father would be horrified
if he thought I was using his tuition dollars
    so recklessly."

A girl who'd come in earlier
    related to the TK family
asked Lisa to remember that I was the youngest.
"She will mature soon enough.
    Stop picking on her."

Lisa reached for my necklace.
I tried to stop her but she got to it first.

In Seed County I always defended Brother.
I did not hold back even with boys.
But I never started a fight, not once.
But what do you do here?
    Fighting is unseemly, Cousin Abigail thinks.
It is just another way to settle a thing in the country
    especially among boys, who I was around mostly.

"Turn it loose," I asked Lisa.

"Say please."

If she was Titus, we'd be in the dust
on the ground outside, rolling around.
But this is not Seed County and she is not Titus.
"Please," I said between tight teeth.

Finally, she turned it loose.

ALONE IN MY CLOSET

I sat in my closet with my things
a long time
thinking what to do about Lisa.
I am her enemy.
    Not that I want to be.

PAYBACK

I sat on the porch
knitting Brother a scarf.
Undoing it all because of my sour mood.
By the time Dorothy showed up
with Lisa right behind her
I had a lap full of yarn
unraveled.
"I saw the scarf you were knitting.
    Who does that?" Dorothy asked.

I thought it was a compliment.
Proud
I told her Gran taught me.
But I never much cared for it.
    Here it comforts me
but I didn't tell her that.

They laughed.
    "I would have thought you'd have the money
to purchase a store-bought one?"

Right then the postman showed up
with an armful of letters and packages.
He came to me straightaway.
    "Since you arrived, young lady
my work has increased tenfold.
Now, let's see—"

Their eyes popped.
He handed me six letters and two packages.
    Lisa wanted to know if there was anything for her.
"No."

Walking off I heard her say, "Did you see how
wrinkled and stained her parcels were?"

There was no truth to it.
But I did find a postcard with my mail
that belonged to her. It was from her dad.
Later, I slipped it under her door
      but not before I read it.

Dearest Daughter,
    Hope all is well.
I will visit you next week I promise.
Life is constantly getting away from me.
Expect a package next month.

Your loving Father

STAMPED FROM THE BEGINNING

Once a month we can go home for the weekend.

Almost every girl left last night except me and Lisa
    and she barely left her room.
    Ma sent me a letter with red-lipstick kisses on it
along with a four-layer coconut cake.
I ate my share in my room with the door closed.
Thought about places to volunteer.
Wished Alabaster would drop by.
He didn't.

Ma's cake was already gone

by the time everyone got back Sunday evening.
    Bert ate two slices sitting cross-legged on her bed.
Alexandria ate one and a half but not before offering me
three of her ribbons.
She noticed I could use a few, she said.
    It felt like home.
Neighbors sharing what they had.

Could I please forgive them, some of them asked.
"Lisa does not want us cavorting with you.
    And her father's influence is wide."

"What does she have against me?"

Alexandria blurted it out.
"It is your pedigree."

"What?"

It was Bert who explained.
    "It is like a stamp on your forehead.
For better or worse, it can seal your fate
    limit your place in society
or lift you high as the sky.
Nothing or no one can change it, some think.
Not even you."

LEAVING MORE THINGS BEHIND

Lying awake I thought about Ma
and how she raised us.
> *You can be what you want in life.*
Climb as high as you wish, she taught Brother and me.
> *Nothing can stop you*
not even pedigree, she'd say.

But how would Ma know
how to get along at a place like this
with girls who travel on ships and planes
or vacation high in the mountains?

I went to my desk
took out my knitting needles and yarn.
In the dark, I worked on Brother's scarf.
Thought better of it
stuck it all in the suitcase.
> Said goodbye for now.

TK

CHANGING DIRECTIONS

LOSING TO LISA AGAIN

During history Mrs. Santiago
said it was time for us to talk about our own families.
That way the other students
would get to know me a wee bit better
and I'd get to know them too.
    Everyone looked my way.
Lisa stood up when I did
but got to the front of the class ahead of me.
    "May I go first, Mrs. Santiago?"

"Why, of course, Lisa."

She talked on and on
reminding me of the lighthouse foghorn back home
screaming into the night
when you wished it would be quiet.

Her family's roots in this city are as deep
    as the Schuylkill River, she told us.

"As if any of us needed reminding," Bert whispered.

    "We have been in Philadelphia nearly since
the beginning. Father says he has plans
to build his own hospital one day
to seal his legacy in stone and glass."
    She sat down mighty satisfied with herself.
Shirley
a girl behind me, leaned forward.
"Isn't she the worst?"

I kept quiet.

    But not her.
"Lisa's father is expected tomorrow.
    But will he come? No.
She will make some excuse
    for his absence, I'm sure."

TAKING MY TURN

I decided to talk about Ma.
How much she loves science and the stars.
How Brother takes after her.
    Plans to be an astronomer.

It got them all talking
raising their hands
    and asking questions
once I brought up the lighthouse in Seed County
    and Brother's last letter.
He wants to be a junior lighthouse keeper next summer.

ONE OF THE GIRLS

It was a first for me at Cousin's school.
Girls on my coattails
    following me up the hall.
How tall is a lighthouse? one asked.
Bert looped her arm through mine.
"Is it true
that some have two hundred steps or more?"

Angel wanted to know if I might have a picture of Brother.
She likes to write to handsome boys, she told us.
We all laughed.

At lunch they sat at my table.
It felt good to be accepted.
    Even if it was only for a little while.

LISA'S TEARS

Lisa sat there all day, darn near
    crying now and then
with girls walking by pretending not to notice.
Me included.
    When Eiffel Tower asked to sit beside her on the porch
Lisa screamed, "I hate you. Go away!"

Once or twice
I saw her on the pavement
walking back and forth
looking up and down the block
checking her Timex watch
    like it would help.
Finally
Cousin came outdoors and brought her in.
    The rest of the week
no one said a word to Lisa.

We knew better.

AN IMITATION OF MYSELF

I got dressed before everyone else.
Went outside to sit on the steps and people watch.

I noticed a girl and her mother across the street.
She goes to work with her
helps her clean houses.
She ought to be in school with us
    she's the right age.
She and her mom
are fresh from the South too
Alabaster told me once.

Truth is
I'm more like her than Lisa and the others;
girls of means
Society-page queens.

Do I really belong here at Cousin's school?
I asked myself. Or am I an imitation?
Fake as the story Lisa's
father made up about coming to visit her.

OFF TO VOLUNTEER

On Sunday Bert sneaked out the house before breakfast.
Wearing pants without socks and carrying an apple in her hand
she hurried up the street like somebody owed her money.

Determined to get to the bottom of things
I followed her past lollygaggers
leaving church services
    some standing on corners chewing the fat
Presbyterians and Baptists alike.

I did my best to keep up with her.
    "Bert. Wait. Where . . . where are you going?"

"To volunteer," she said, not slowing down.
    She stepped into the street
jumped back when a trolley turned the corner with the bell
clanging.

"I'll go with you . . ."

"Another time. I promise," she said.

THE GIRL IN FRONT OF OUR SCHOOL

On my way back
I smelled Sunday supper everywhere.
Fried chicken.
    Liver with onions.
Stew of one kind or another.
Cakes and pies
sitting outside on window ledges.

Back at school
I saw that woman and that girl again
this time staring up at our building.

The girl took her mother's hand.
"One day I'll be a student here, right, Mom?"

"Right."

"You promised. Didn't you, Mom?"
    "I promised."

"And you never break a promise."

"I never do."

I stuck my hand out. Said I was new here.
"My name is Hattie Mae."
We shook hands.
    "My name is Adelaide," the girl told me.
"I'm eleven. We hail from Alabama."
    I stared at their shoes.

Adelaide's mom told me to call her Mrs. Carolyn.

"We've been here six months.
Live on South Street, the Seventh Ward.
Work on this block." Mrs. Carolyn pointed across the street.
"One day I'll own one of these houses."

DRUMMING UP CUSTOMERS

Alabaster joined us on the sidewalk.
Staring at that woman's feet
he asked who waxed and repaired her shoes.
She barely got the answer out
    before he handed her a card.
"Ma gives discounts to first-time customers."

ME AND THE MAYOR OF PHILADELPHIA

We sat on the steps, chitchatting
with Alabaster asking me
what I knew about the neighborhood.
Not happy with my answers
    he took to his bike.
Called himself
the mayor of Philadelphia.
"I know where everything is
    and where everybody lives.
Come and see."

Like an explorer
    Christopher Columbus
or Edward Rose
he pointed up and down the block.
Said if I ever got lost
to remember Christian Street nearest us
runs east and west
between Twentieth Street on the one end
    and South Broad on the other.

I stopped.
Took it all in.
Sidewalks wide and clean.
The First African Baptist Church holding up one corner
Edwin Stanton Elementary School and Allmond's Funeral
Home
a stone's throw away.
    And people everywhere.
Most of 'em smiling.
One lady had on a nurse's uniform
    and a starched white cap on her head.

Alabaster stopped his bike
    waved both hands.
"Dr. Jerrick Over here!
It's me. Alabaster.
I shined those shoes you're wearing."

A man in a gray suit and a vest
    came over to us.
"Why, Alabaster. Hello.
It is always a pleasure to see you."

"This is Miss Hattie.
I'm introducing her to the neighborhood."

"I am not at all surprised.
    Hello, young lady."

His office is close by, I learned.
Girls from our school get treated there
for colds
and mumps
bumps and bruises,
he said, with such kindness it made me wish for home.
    "Well, I'm off to the post office, Alabaster."
He turned to me next. "You are in the best of hands
Miss Hattie." And off he went.

Alabaster looked proud of himself.
"Those shoes of Doc's
sure look mighty handsome on his feet," he said.

"They do.
    So shiny too."

"I earned a nickel tip for that."

Alabaster stopped .
This time outside a shoe-repair store.
I so wished it was an ice cream parlor
to help me beat the heat.

Soon as his ma came to the city, he told me
she'd met Mr. Wilson. "This here's his shop.
Ma knew a thing or two about shoes
when she first got here.
But he filled in many a gap.
Taught her to make shoes from scraps of leather.
    He'll have his own shoe-repair school
one day, I'm sure of it.
A chain of 'em, Ma thinks."

We were set to take off again
when a funeral procession
    showed up across the street.
All those people.
Too many feet and shoes to count.
Was too much for Alabaster to resist.
    "Miss Hattie, I got business to attend to.
Hope you don't mind."

WHAT HAPPENED
THE DAY I WENT EXPLORING

I went home
    but didn't stay long.
I just couldn't.
I was too filled up inside.

Toting my pencil
and a notebook full of paper
I slipped out the back door.
Went wherever my feet took me
    just like Alabaster would.

Miles and miles away
turning in circles
I found myself near Boathouse Row.
    What a sight.
Houses with racks of canoes in the back.
People walking slow and easy in the grass.
Trees everywhere.

I flopped down in a mountain of leaves
    close to the river's edge.
Drew a map
with roads and bridges on it
statues and buildings
people on the Schuylkill River
    paddling canoes in both directions.

I stood up to go home
got lost along the way
    then detoured by a crowd
making a ruckus outside a movie theater.

I peeked between arms and elbows.
Squeezed in between a man and a woman.
    "Don't they make you proud?"
the lady said, making room for me.

There they were.
Five picketers holding up signs.
    Bert was one of 'em.

WHAT BERT WAS UP TO ALL ALONG

Do not support this theater, Bert's sign said.
They refuse to hire us as
concessions workers
managers
ticket takers
film rollers.
    WE CAN DO THE JOB. JUST GIVE US A CHANCE.
    another sign read.

Bert shouted, "Jobs now. Jobs now and always."
Waved her sign high in the air.

I sneaked off before she saw me.
    Followed my map home.
Thought about Bert's people
    they would be proud of her, I think.

THE NEWS OF THE DAY

After supper
we're supposed to report our own news
or something we read about
in the last month or two.

Mrs. Dreamer served us warm pumpkin pie
with a scoop of pecan ice cream on top
while we discussed—

The recession.
War approaching.
Jews in Germany asking for help but not getting much.
Jim Crow, who is on the table every night, rain or shine
to be poked and sliced
carved and picked clean
until he's gone for good
     Cousin insists.

I put my fork and knife on my plate
    the way she taught me
one lying across the other
both face down.
    I raised my hand.
"1938 is the
    year of our Golden Jubilee."

I looked at Cousin at the other end of the table.
She smiled. "Please continue."

"I read it in *Time* magazine.
    The jubilee celebrates
the seventy-fifth year our people

been out of slavery." I reached for my fork.
"That's all I have to say."

Lisa looked discontented.
    "It was hardly worth noting. Slavery was
a long time ago. And some of our families were
never bought nor paid for."

Cousin took it from there, asking the others
how they felt about what was said
and ways they could add to the conversation.
We sat there another fifteen minutes.
Most people agreeing with me
that the jubilee was worth mentioning
celebrating even.

BERT A MOVIE STAR

Our bedroom
is the ocean we can go to
whenever we please
day or night
    to find peace,
Bert likes to say.

At my desk
I colored
and wished I hadn't stashed
my knitting needles.

From her side of the room
    Bert interrupted me.
"Can you keep a secret?"

I set my crayon down.
Sure, I said, hoping
    she would tell me about last Sunday afternoon at the
    movies.
Smiling from ear to ear, she ran to her desk.
Pulled open the bottom drawer.
Came over to me with an armful
of black-and-white photographs.
    Carefully
she set them on my bed.

"I want to be an actress.
Famous one day, like her and her and her."
She pointed to Billie Holiday with a gardenia in her hair.
Ethel Waters at a microphone, wailing.

Lena Horne at the Cotton Club, dancing
    smiling and sweating.

Bert looked sad.
"My father tells me I'll be an actress
    over his dead body."

POEM TITLE TK

Bert's father has three secretaries
six agents
and four apartment buildings he rents.
They live in a mansion
    spend summers in a second house at Oak Bluffs.
Bert is the oldest.
He wants her to take over
his insurance business one day.
His office is across town.
There's another one in New York City.
He wears a gold watch and suits with vests, she told me.
    Insists that Bert go to Spelman
then Tuskegee for a second degree
like so many in her family.

"After I graduate
I have to work for him.
My father will make me.
    But I couldn't bear it."

"Then tell him no."

"No one refuses my father."

For the rest of the afternoon
    she pasted photos on the wall.
I worked on my quilt.
    Took out Gran's favorite tin
        filled with needles, pins, thimbles and thread
taking my time sewing the patches on.
Then we heard him, Alabaster
yelling our names from outside.

Pitching rocks at our window
to get our attention.

For the rest of the day
we chased behind him and his bike
having more fun than we could count.

THE WORST FATHER EVER

Lisa came to math class late
    almost tripped over my feet.
She blamed it on me
    but she went out of her way
to make sure it happened.
    "Apologize," she said.

I almost did
just to avoid getting into more trouble.
But Mrs. Grable interrupted us.
"Lisa. To the office."
    "It wasn't my fault!"
    "I have a note. It says your father is here to visit with you."
She wrote her a hall pass. "Quickly. I'm told he
hasn't much time."
    Lisa flew out the room.

None of us could stay in our seats.
    We wondered out loud what he might look like.
How long he'd stay. If he came with presents.
Mrs. Grable clapped her hands. "Ladies, please."
But she was at the window too.
    Twenty minutes later Antoinette walked in.
Did she see Lisa's father? we asked.
    Did they hug? Leave the building?
    Lisa's father never left the car,
        she said from the front of the room.
As far as she could tell he never invited
her inside to chat either.
    "She stood there like a stranger
talking to him through the window."

"How awful," Mrs. Grable said. It slipped out, we could tell.

GRAN'S ADVICE

I sat down
wrote a letter to Gran about Lisa.
How I never raised a finger to her
after she came back to class
scowling and yelling at me
    like I'd done something to her.

Gran is old but quick.
She got back to me in a hurry.
    Seems like Lisa's father's got his own troubles, she wrote.
Something he don't want that child to know about.
    But nonetheless do not let her alter your course
    or make a fool outta you.

In the meantime, keep your chin up.

GOOD TIMES WITH BERT

Every week
I share a letter with Bert
who likes to hear what my family is up to
loves the things they send in the mail
    like homemade baked goods from Ma
ten squares
once a month from Gran.
    By the end of the school year
I'll have enough patches
to sew together and make my own quilt.

Pastor's wife surprised me.
Sends ten cents once a month
along with a short note.
    She sure likes to chew on gossip.

Sitting across her
Bert listened to me read Gran's letter
while she licked peppermint sticks
    Gran sent to her especially.

Bring Bert down here sometime.
We'll spoil her rotten, she wrote.

Bert was ready to hear Brother's letter next.
    He didn't send one this week
or last. That isn't like him.

MAKING THE GRADE

The house was quiet.
Dark.
I was at my desk.
The only one awake.

We had a spelling test the next day
forty-five words
some I'd never heard of before.
I made flash cards
picked one up
shut my eyes
spelled the word under my breath.
Picked up the next card.
Stumbled over a letter or two.
Wrote it down ten times
    went to the next spelling word.
Country life makes you strong,
Gran says. "Quitting ain't in our blood."

When she handed my paper back
Mrs. Grable told me to watch my handwriting.
"Otherwise—" Her thumb went up.
    "You are one smart cookie, Hattie Mae."

I made 100 percent.
    Lisa said that was the least I could do.

COUSIN'S NEWS

On the bulletin board outside of class
Cousin Abigail posted a notice.
Next week
the board would meet at our school.
Beforehand
there would be a reception.
She wanted all of us to attend
and make a good impression.

I went hunting in my closet for a dress.
Found one Daddy bought last year.
It would do.

ALL DRESSED UP

Every stall in the bathroom was full.
More girls stood in front of the sinks
    staring at themselves in the mirrors.

They were giggling
running in and out of the bathroom
asking everybody's opinion about their hair
    the color of their nails
pancake make-up on their faces
    that Cousin said they weren't to wear.

I stood at the bathroom door, watching.
    "Hattie. Hurry. Tie my bow."
Bert turned her back to me. "It's so exciting.
I hear they will serve filet mignon.
Have you ever had it? Yum." She rubbed her belly.

"Be still."
I started the bow over again.
"I've had all sorts of meat. Even lamb and venison.
It's all the same, I think.
    It's the cook that makes the dish."

Once I was done
Bert grabbed my hand and took off running.

The hall was a highway of girls
trying not to crash into each other.
    "Excuse me."
        "Sorry."
"Goodness. This isn't very ladylike."

Bert sat at the vanity.
I took out her hair rollers
combed her hair with my fingers.
 Ignored her when she asked
when I was getting dressed.

"Soon."

"You will come, won't you?"

"I said I would."

She offered me her dress again.
The one in her closet that she never wore.
Mine will do just fine,
I told her.
Not that I was 100 percent sure.
But my father bought it so I was wearing it
no matter what.

INTRODUCING MISS ABIGAIL'S GIRLS

They looked like sherbet ice cream
in their pink and purple dresses
salmon, eggnog and mint green gowns.
    Bert's baby blue shoes sparkled. Lisa had on a crown.
Angelina wore cutouts dyed to match her outfit—lime green.
No lining up that night. They took the stairs two at a time.
Cousin was to announce each girl as she arrived in the drawing room
where the reception was.
But not me.
I was the last to get dressed.
    The last to put on gloves
to walk downstairs and get introduced.
Oh, the looks I got.

DRESSING

My dress was plain white, lace
    scalloped on the bottom.
The gloves were yellow
up to my elbows.
    The only thing I borrowed from Bert.

In the bathroom I took a brush to my hair
scooped it into a big, soft, puffy ball.
I liked how I looked.
    "Here goes, Hattie Mae."

I could hear Brother cheering me on.

HOBNOBBING WITH THE UPPER CRUST

I was on my way downstairs
when I heard Cousin thanking everyone for attending.
"As our board, I hope you will see via our girls that your time
and donations were well invested.
    Please, enjoy yourselves. Our young ladies are exceptional
indeed."

The dress I had on was sleeveless.
Meant for summer.
But it was the closest to a formal dress I owned.
Daddy lit up when he paid for it.
    It deserved a spin around the room.

I walked over to the first grown-up I saw
Mrs. Wintergarden.
"Hello, I'm Hattie Mae," I said, extending my hand.
"I know who you are. The *Tribune* writes about you.
And Miss Abigail speaks highly of you."

She shook my hand. But didn't say much.
    I was glad when Mr. Gage showed up
with a tray of hors d'oeuvres in his hand
and a wink for me. Mrs. Wintergarden waved him off.
I took what was offered, pigs in a blanket
    celery filled with pimentos and cream
a champagne flute with something bubbly inside
Canada Dry soda.

Cousin wanted us to engage in small talk, she said
    to ask board members about their health, charity efforts
or summer plans.

I asked Mrs. Wintergarden about the weather.
Bert, close by, asked Mrs. Helen the same question.

I brought up other charities Mrs. Wintergarden was involved with.
    "However did you know?" she asked.

"Reading and research. I enjoy both."

For generations her family has believed in philanthropic efforts like these.
It's how all boats ride, she said, sipping on seltzer water.
Then she threw a question my way.
    "What do you think of the school?"

I didn't have to make up an answer.
It was sitting on the tip of my tongue.
    "Every child should attend here for at least a year.
It makes you feel important
plus you learn a lot."

I never knew I felt that way until I said it out loud.

I waited for Bert to repeat after me.
She didn't.
She got quiet.
Then she blurted it out.
"This school is the best thing to ever happen to me.
I have grown exponentially.
I still have a long way to go.
But once I become a famous actor . . ."
She smiled like cameras were flashing around her.
    ". . . everyone will know I attended Miss Abigail's School.
And that I am an exceptional girl."

She bowed like she could hear applause.
    That's the only reason I clapped.
It seemed like the right thing to do.
Mrs. Helen clapped too.
    So did a few others.

"It might be better if she chose
a different profession," I overheard one board member say.
"A life on the stage is a poor excuse for a career.
So many end up on skid row seeking fame."

"You shouldn't say that!"
It slipped out.
    "It took a lot of courage for Bert to speak up.
And no one has the right to squash your dreams."
    Cousin asked me to leave.
To go to my room.
I went outside instead
    and sat on the steps.

THAT GIRL AND HER MOM AGAIN

"Are they having a party in there?" Adelaide asked.
"I like parties." She was on her tiptoes trying to get a good look inside.

"Mom works for Mr. Benjamin. Do you know him?"

Before I could say no
    the door opened.
Lucky for me it wasn't Cousin.
I introduced Bert. She shared a brownie with the girl.

"We ought to go in. Miss Abigail wants us to sing for them."

"Not me, I'm sure."

"She sent me to get you.
    Mrs. Wintergarden insisted."

"Me?"

"She said you had spunk."

PRACTICE MAKES PERFECT

I sang the loudest
but there were no complaints.
In fact Cousin and Mrs. Wintergarden complimented me.
Afterward we were all dismissed
free to do as we pleased.

I went upstairs
worked on walking tall and straight like Cousin's social club
members.

I walked back and forth in the hall
      with a book on my head
  the encyclopedia
section D–F, which is no small thing.
    "Ridiculous." Lisa hurried by me.
"Some of us are trying to sleep."
Eiffel Tower slammed her door shut.
    Bert encouraged me.
"There are still twenty minutes to go
before lights out."
She got to her feet
found a book in our room and joined in.
    "Did she really say it? That I had spunk?"

Bert nodded.
    Lisa's door flew open.
"I hope you discard that dress. It is horrid."
    Later in bed I asked Bert's opinion.
It's pretty enough, she told me.
But not appropriate for entertaining bigwigs.
    "You want to be important one day.

A person of distinction, right?"
"Right."
"Well, clothes do matter. Lisa is correct about that."

GETTING RID OF THINGS THAT NO LONG SUIT ME

Into the suitcase the dress went
with a few other things
    bobby socks a wee bit too small
my crinoline slip
the patches Gran sends
    rag ties for my hair at night
a paisley skirt and a sweater out of fashion
pajamas
    itchy and wool.
I'd rather sleep in my birthday suit.

A DAY FILLED WITH HARD WORK AND SURPRISES

Alabaster told me he's been working long and hard
    which is why we haven't seen him around.
He held out his hand.
    "I picked 'em for you."
He had a handful of acorns
and golden-brown leaves.

I took what I wanted
and skipped off to class.

Lisa shook her head when she saw me.
Bert sniffed and smiled.
Mrs. Britain asked if I had an admirer.
    "She sure does," Bert told her.

I kept quiet.
Pulled out my notebook
protractor and pencil.

"Who did the assignment?"
    Mrs. Britain walked the classroom.
"Hattie asked the question last week.
    It was an excellent one, indeed.
Who invented the protractor?"
    She held one up.

"A monster," Bert said.
    "We get enough work without
that device."

I didn't know the answer.

I ought to have. But I kept falling asleep
doing my homework assignments.

Mrs. Britain stopped at my desk.
Looked down at me.

"I know." Lisa's hand went up.
    Was it a trick?
But she did know.
    "Thomas Blundeville invented it to measure angles."
    "Great answer. But do consider this as well. The Egyptians were master builders, knowledgeable at geometry and math," she told us. "All of those pyramids and angles . . . they had to use something to measure them. I would not be surprised if they had a hand in the invention as well . . . even four or five thousand years ago."

She always has something interesting to add
to our lessons.
We were to draw our own pyramids and measure the angles,
area and volume
    then come up with a math problem based on what we discovered.
We all got right to work. What fun, truly.

BANKING ON MY OWN MONEY

Soon as Lisa left the teller line
at the Citizens and Southern Bank, I stepped up.
Set my money on the counter.
Ten cents.
And handed over my passbook.
The teller wrote down the amount I was depositing.
And smiled. "Your balance is six dollars and twenty-five cents.
That's a lot for a little girl. Any plans for it?"

"I need new clothes," I told her.
"So, I'm saving up."

Cousin and Mr. Wright, the bank president
sat in his office, talking
and drinking coffee. He used to be on her board.
Before we left he asked how things were going.
"Fair to middlin'," she told him.

He gave her a contribution.
Said he believed in our school and her mission.
"Keep up the good work."

SURPRISE, SURPRISE

Bert and me were all set to go window shopping
    when someone knocked on the door.
    Our mouths dropped at the sight of
the box in the mailman's hand.
It was taller than me.
Burgundy
with white velvet ribbons tied like
and flowers in the middle that smelled like carnations.
    It was from one of the most exclusive shops in the city,
Cousin Abigail told us. "Lisa! Someone go get her."

Bert volunteered.
Cousin reached for the card on the box
stopped and stared at me.
    "There's been a mistake. It's . . . it's for you, Hattie Mae."

ME AND MY FANCY NEW DRESS

It sat in a sea of satin
the same color as the box.
I didn't want to touch it.
    Bert said I had to.
"Mrs. Wintergarden went to such trouble."

Cousin read the note that came with it
just when Lisa walked in.
    "Keep striving but know thyself always."

MAYBE LISA IS RIGHT ABOUT ME

I got up early and sneaked into my new gown
    zipping it up without help.
    Barefooted
hair asunder
    I stepped into the hallway.
Stared at myself in the mirror a long, long time.
I liked this Hattie Mae.

The hardwood floors were chilly under my feet.
But I did not let that stop me.
Down the stairs I went.
    Waving like Princess Elizabeth.

Lifting my gown high
I went to the kitchen
    ended up in the parlor
serving myself water in a china cup
almond cookies made the day before
and a handful of raisins.

It was Lisa who found me asleep.
    She called me a social climber.
Said my dress was proof of it. She brought up
my table manners
the night of the board members' dinner
    how rude I was to one of them.
"You are all show and pretense.
    A charity case to Mrs. Wintergarden.
It will all come out in the wash.
They'll see."

I stood taller. "See what?"

"That you're a freeloader.
Why, I bet you don't even pay tuition."

My whole body turned to stone.
    I couldn't move a finger or say a word.

"Aha! It *is* true. And you know it."
That's when she called me a thief.
    Said by attending school tuition-free
I was stealing from the other girls.
    "Wait until Father hears."

"I'll make it up to the school!"
    "How?"
    "I don't know, but I will."

CHARITY NOT WANTED

Into the suitcase it went
    Mrs. Wintergarden's gown.
Even though wearing it
I felt like an angel
like I had earned the right to be here.
But I am no one's charity case.
Mrs. Wintergarden could keep her handouts.

PAYING MY WAY

I thought about James Henry
Gran
Seed County
me toting milk to the house in a tin pail.

On the farm
we all did our part.
No freeloaders there
or charity cases
just family
neighbors looking out for neighbors
all of us working together
not expecting anything in return.
In the dark
I sat up
wishing I was there again
gathering eggs
shelling peas
walking up dirt roads with Lottie Jean
barefooted and happy.

By the time morning came
I had it figured out.
I'd pay my own way
the best way I knew how.
Not in dollars and cents
    but with good old-fashioned elbow grease.

TK

DOING THINGS MY WAY

WORKING DAY AND NIGHT TO SET THINGS RIGHT

Before the other girls woke up
or Mr. Gage and Mrs. Dreamer got to work
I grabbed a pail and a sponge
mopped the bathroom floor on my knees.

The pine oil took me back to Gran's.
Made me feel useful
like I was earning my keep.

*Hard work
ain't nothing to be ashamed of,*
Gran would say.
But oh did my knees ache.

"Hattie!"
Bert walked in, rubbing her eyes.
"What are you doing?
    Why are you up this early?"

I put my finger up. "Hush."
Stood up
told her my plan.
"If I prove that I deserve to be here
that I'm not on the dole—"

"You do deserve to be here!"

"Some don't think so."

I shared part of my secret with her
that Miss Abigail lets me attend for free.
    Sticking out her hand

she asked for the sponge.
"Let me help."

"No thank you.
    It's my debt to pay."

SLEEPING WHILE I EAT

I was last getting dressed for school.
Last joining the line in the hall and
    finishing my breakfast too.
I ate
with one hand on my lap
the other one holding my head up
my elbow on the table
    which Lisa told me about.

My fingers were wrinkled from the hot water
and too much scrubbing.

Lisa commented on my hair.
    Steam from the radiator in the bathroom
shrunk it.

KEEPING SECRETS FOR ONE ANOTHER

After school
the second week in a row
I flew upstairs to my room.
Pulled open my drawer
took out a good pencil
    and got to work.
Bert and I usually
do arithmetic at the same time
but not today, I told her.
    "I have chores to do."

"Miss Abigail has been asking about you.
She wonders where you disappear to.
    I tell her you're walking the neighborhood
doing homework in the park. How long can you keep it up?"

"I don't know.
But what about you?
You disappear too."

And I know where, I almost added.
But her face looked so sad
and disappointed.
I didn't push any further.

THE MAID

Mr. Gage quit walking.
Backed up.
Came inside the library on the second floor.

I meant to close the door
    so no one would see me working.

"Girl
what's that in your hand?"

I hid the feather duster behind my back.
He stuck his hand out.
Kept it there
insisted I turn it over to him.
I did.

"You trying to step into my position?"

"No, sir."

He asked why I wasn't outdoors
playing in the sun
or in here reading
studying
filling my head with knowledge.

"Don't tell Cousin . . . I mean . . . Miss Abigail."
I stared at my feet. "Please . . ."

Bending to my height
he said my secret was safe with him.
    "I knew all along." He winked

lifted my chin till my eyes met his.
"You look related
like kin.
If people paid enough attention, they'd see."

I say it again.
"Do not tell . . . please don't.
It might cost Cousin more than she ought to pay."

"If that Lisa knew, it would cost the whole school.
Lordy, she sure is hard on the world."

"Sure is." I laughed.

"But hardest on herself, I'd say."

"Cousin says something similar."

"Never you mind."
He stood up. "When fortune smiles on you
accept it. And rise above your station.
I have."

For the first time I noticed
his fingernails
chipped low, always
buffed and shiny.
His uniform pants creased just so
with cuffs turned up the same length
on both legs.
A crisp white shirt
black tie
a belt buckle shining like an August moon.
A clean-shaven face

a straight back that seemed like
it never knew a day's work
or stooped low to hoe
pull up tobacco
or force cotton to do his bidding.

Proud as the lions outside the bank
he walked out with the duster
whistling.

PUSHING MYSELF

In spite of Mr. Gage's words
I took care of a few more chores.
Finally
I sat down on the porch in the fall sun.
Bert went off to protest
I'm sure.
Slouching
wondering what I should do next,
I saw Alabaster coming up the sidewalk on his bike.
"You are the least fun girl I know, Miss Hattie."

I stood up and stomped my feet.
"I am fun, Alabaster!"

"Then come."
He went to his bike and patted the seat.

I stood still.

"Another time."

"I'll pay you a nickel if you ride with me,"
    Alabaster said, like he had one to spare.

I'd never ridden on a bike before
but didn't let on.
Still
in my head I heard James Henry say,
"Ah, go on, Sister.
    What harm can it cause?"

FUN

Back
in Seed County, North Carolina
I had lots of fun.

Since leaving, I've concluded that
Brother drummed up most of it.

Because of him
we built rocket ships
blasted off to space
made the roof a bed and the stars our friends
fought aliens
walked across galaxies barefooted.
He saved me a time or two
    and me, him.

We both had our fears
only I never let on with Ma ailing.
I had to be strong
a grown-up nearly.
    Which is one reason I longed
to come to Philadelphia.

It seemed a body could be themselves here.
Not a twin
or double of anyone or anything.

Now
that I'm here
it wears on me
to be so far away from my family.
To be so unliked

by girls who look like me.

A FUN GIRL LIKE ME

Determined to be a fun girl
    I sat on the bike
behind Alabaster.
Held on to his waist
    tight as husk holds corn.

He took off.
Jumped the curb
rode the bike till the sidewalk ran out
then
back onto the cobblestone street we went
crooked sometimes
till he
found another sidewalk to ride up
another curb to jump over.

Before I knew it, Alabaster hollered
"Hold on tighter
    if you know what's good for ya."
I did.

The wind
pushed my bangs into my eyes.
Made 'em water.
My head went forward
    hitting his back.
I ended up seeing stars
    but I was smiling anyhow.
For a minute I thought about Brother
    and Seed County.
Together we could do anything.

SEEING THINGS THROUGH ALABASTER'S EYES

I shut my eyes
listened
to the sounds all around me on South Street.
Trolley bells ringing
car horns
cab drivers stuck in traffic
mad.
People shopping in stores and on sidewalks
buying potatoes by the pound, apples from barrows, fish
hanging on hooks
two-dollar suits for men, used pots and pans, live chickens in
crates by the curb.

On we went
passing full buses
men with jackhammers breaking up the ground
     women holding pocketbooks
red
blue
brown
gray
past row house after row house
     so many in need of repair
women sitting in chairs on sidewalks
     one rubbing her knee
     two reading *The Daily News*
     another yawning
     a granny singing while she swept.

Alabaster whizzed past his house
     waving. Four families share one bathroom in his building

he said. "We eat our meals together every Sunday. Family is what you make it, Mom taught me."

He turned the corner in a flash. I held on tighter.

"Having fun yet?" Alabaster asked.

"More than I have in a long while."

HOME AGAIN

Alabaster wanted to know if I knew that I was pretty.
Of course.
Ma
and Daddy
tell me all the time.
Plus, I got eyes.
But kind words are always appreciated.

"Thank you, Alabaster."
    He mentioned shoes for some reason.
Said something about free ones.

For me? I asked.
I could use another pair.

People don't always pick them up at the shop,
he told me.
"There's a red pair at the shop, never paid for. Likely your size.
I think you should have them, Miss Hattie."

I leaned in closer
let him know I could not possibly take a gift from a boy
without asking permission first.
But who would I ask?
Cousin Abigail or Ma?

Right then
his bike wobbled.

"Careful," I told him.

He's the best biker in the world, he said.

"Watch."

He crossed the street
    pedaled like his feet were light as feathers.
Up he went with the bike
over a suitcase set on the sidewalk
for tomorrow's trash.
I was surprised we both didn't die.

A TERRIBLE END
TO A VERY GOOD DAY

Alabaster wasn't content.
A few blocks from school
pedaling faster and faster
he aimed for more trash sitting on a corner
two metal cans
     one beside the other.
     "Let me off!
Take me home!"

"We can make it, Miss Hattie.
I promise."

If promises were pennies
     we'd all be rich, Gran says.

Not a second later
I ended up on the ground
beside Alabaster's
upside-down bike
     the wheels spinning.

He jumped up quick.
     Asked if I was okay.

I lost a shoe.
My elbow was bruised
     bleeding.

My slip ripped.
My sweater sleeve torn.

My palms scratched.

Alabaster turned a perfectly good day
into a mess.

LIMPING MY WAY HOME

He offered to walk me home.
"You did enough," I said
limping up the block.

I stopped every few houses.
Rubbed my knee.
Kicked myself
because I ought to have known better.

Accidents.
Injuries.
Tomfoolery of every sort
are supposed to be reported to Cousin Abigail
who will write a report
and send it home to your family.

BERT TO THE RESCUE

Bert showed up out of nowhere
just in the nick of time.
    I explained my predicament to her.

She said she would be a decoy
distract Cousin Abigail, sitting on the porch
    in the shade, reading *Ladies' Home Journal.*

"Miss Abigail!" Bert bounced across the street.
"May I ask you a question
    about my class assignment?"

"Why, certainly."

Bert brought up
an arithmetic problem
she claimed to have difficulty solving.

Cousin
is eager to help always.
"Oh, of course.
    Now is a perfect time," she told Bert.

Bert
explained that her notebook was inside the house.

"Well, then
we should get to it quickly."

GETTING WHAT I CAME HERE FOR

"Don't tell,"
I said, hobbling past Lisa on the stairs.

She beat me to my room.
Turned the doorknob and stepped back.
    "Look at yourself.
Getting into scraps.
You will never be first-rate
    You do not belong here.
And you know it."

I thought about what Mr. Gage said, and Ma.
"I came for an education.
Like you and everyone else.
You should want every girl to learn."

They were Ma's words
    changed a bit to suit the situation.
Told to Titus's father
who refused to let him return to school
after planting season was done.

Lisa didn't have anything to say for once.

After she went downstairs
Bert came in with a bottle of iodine
cotton balls in an apothecary jar
along with bandages and gauze.
I was thankful to her for fixing me up.

MY PRETTY FANCY RED SHOES

By day's end
with the moon out
there they were
on the front porch
red shoes
    exactly my size.

Shiny
just about new
with a side buckle that could fool you for real gold.

Dear Miss Hattie Mae,
    I hope your ma will let you accept these shoes.
    I polished them three times
especially for you.

I figure it won't do no harm to accept 'em.

HOLDING BACK THE TRUTH

My shoes made quite
    a fuss.
Nearly every girl reminded me
I was not dressed according to code.
Usually, we wear white saddle shoes.

Cousin Abigail didn't mind
because she never saw them on my feet.
I was last in line.
Last at the table
    and last to leave.

I marched into class, proud
like I had a band playing behind me.
    Made a beeline to my seat.

Mrs. Britain hurried over.
Asked what was going on with my chin.
"Nothing."
    She cleared her throat.

"Not a thing, Mrs. Britain."

Her face never moves.
Always looks stern
even if she's in a chipper mood.
"Well
it looks as if you have taken a terrible
tumble."

"I'm fine." I sat down

tried to hide the Band-Aid
on my knee.

"Fisticuffs and rowdiness
are grounds for expulsion, you know."

"I tripped and fell, that's all. For real."
I raised my hand. "Honest to goodness."

She glared at my feet.
"During lunch
please relieve yourself of those, young lady.
    We have dress codes, you know."

DOING WHAT I KNOW I SHOULDN'T

Last week I shared one of Gran's cookies
with the mailman.
    Today he gave me Lisa's mail on purpose.
Postcards.
Including one from her stepmother.

I went upstairs to change my shoes
slid her postcards under her door.
But not before I read them.
All three.
This time sitting down.

Her stepmother was headed to Africa, I learned.
    She didn't know when she might return.
Her father was canceling his Thanksgiving visit.
He just couldn't get away from work.

Done reading
I slid the postcards under her door
noticed it was ajar.
    I just had to go in.

A STORM BREWING

I expected her room to look different.
Like a showroom in a department store
    racks of beautiful dresses in the closet
shirts folded on shelves.
Everything neat and tidy.
Instead
fur coats littered the floor like rubbish.
Dresses
    piled high on a Queen Anne chair
were wrinkled and uncared for
in every color and fabric
polka-dot
plaid
satin and silk
herringbone and striped
cotton with crinoline slips and lace.
Most still had tags.
    I did my best to step around them.

LOSING A PART OF ME

Lisa's bed wasn't any better.
It was full of coats and hats, scarves and gloves
mismatched mittens.

I stood at attention
eyeballed the rest of the room.
Perfumes and powders, lotions and brushes
took up the whole dresser.
Papers and inkwells sat on her desk
next to parchment paper in every color.

Turning
I felt my necklace fall off.
"Gran's ring—"

With the twine in my hand
I got down on my knees.
Slid underneath her four-poster bed.
    Not that it did any good.

Standing up
    dusting myself off
I heard somebody talking outside the door.
Lisa and Eiffel Tower.
    "Come to my room, Lisa.
I have photos of my parents at an event with the mayor.
The Tribune interviewed her and Crystal Bird Fauset, our
legislator.
Mother loves that sort of thing, you know."

WHAT I FOUND OUT ABOUT LISA

Out the side of my eye

I saw something shiny underneath her dresser.
Found it along with a letter
balled up tight.

It was Lisa's ring, not Gran's.
And I couldn't believe my eyes—
    the letter was from Cousin Abigail
addressed to Lisa's father.
I couldn't believe it.
    I had to sit myself down to read it.

Dear Dr. Connolly:
    I believe Lisa may be depressed.
Her room certainly shows signs of it.
Her behavior too.
She is sour day and night
troubling one little girl whose only crime
was to attend our school with limited resources
and a Southern address.

For the first time I felt like Cousin was on my side.
    I learned a little bit about Lisa too.
But how did she wind up with this letter?

RIGHT BACK WHERE I STARTED

I couldn't sleep, thinking about Gran's ring.
I tossed and I turned, holding on to the string
that went along with it.

Finally I got up in the middle of the night
sneaked out of my room.
Down South
we know how to move so even a cricket
can't tell you're close.

I opened Lisa's door.
Saw her sleeping.
Was all set to go in when Bert stopped me.
"Go back to bed, Hattie.
What is done is done."
    "But you don't know what happened.
"Gran's ring is lost in there."

"For spite, Lisa will make sure
you never get it back. We should leave."

Lisa yawned
turned her back to us.

I closed the door.
Wondered why girls like her
keep winning.

LYING TO LISA
FOR AS LONG AS I CAN

After that night I noticed Lisa

looking at me like she knew

I'd been up to no good.
     "You will not get away with it, Hattie,"
she said the next day.
I thought about the ring. Wondered if she found it.

But I kept pretending. "What did I do?"

"Something. I feel it."

Maybe she knew I'd been in her room
the night before. Or was it about the postcards?
At dinner
she asked who put them on her dresser.
     So she wouldn't suspect me
Bert said she saw Mr. Gage do it.
Lisa never tried to get to the bottom of things.

Raising my hand to distract her
I asked Cousin Abigail about
the list of places we could volunteer.
     "Will it be posted soon?"

Out of nowhere, Cousin Abigail put me in charge of things.
I was to ask the other students
to give me names for the list.
"Mrs. Grable will let you all cast votes on the top picks after

Thanksgiving.
    And take it from there."

After class Bert said I needed not bother with her.
"There's a nursing home for old veterans
    near the theater. I volunteer there."

TELLING FIBS

My map is always with me.
I pulled it out of my purse
followed it
penciling in new places.
Ended up at the theater in no time.
Bert wasn't on the protest line.
Or at the nursing home.
    Folks there said they'd never heard of her.

CLEANING UP FOR GUESTS

The first Saturday in November I kept to myself.
The other girls went every which way
    to the movies
    the hairdresser
    and Marion's Tearoom.
    Mr. Gage drove them.

Bert's father picked her up
said he could use her help with some filing
in his office.

Cousin put me to work
determined
I was wasting a perfectly good Saturday
reading the society pages
making lists of the latest styles.

I helped her dress the table
make the food
    finger sandwiches
made with sardines and olives
ham and Swiss cheese on rye
a Jell-O salad with pretzels in it
a bowl of tangerines
nuts on pretty plates.
    I even got to make the coffee.

Cousin handed me two dollars.
Said it was a tip.

ME AND THE WOMEN
OF THE FUTURE CLUB

The women of the Future Club
    remind me of Gran and her friends.
But instead of carrying knitting needles and
yarn in their bags
or rocking on porches
    laughing and gossiping
they walked in the house carrying briefcases
wearing suits
cat-eye glasses
looking serious and put together.

I
    peeked between the spindles
on the stairs
listened and watched.

There were two lawyers
a pediatrician
one nurse from Douglass Hospital, one from Mercy
a housewife whose husband was a surgeon
three women who had their own businesses
    a dressmaker
    a horse-riding instructor
    a grocery store owner from North Philly
social workers
a librarian.
One woman from Harlem, another from Jersey
a third from Germantown by way of Delaware
the rest born in the Seventh Ward, North and West Philly.
One from Barbados, even.
I know

because they had a new member
and Cousin had the old ones
introduce themselves.

They talked about a man named Robert
who has a lot of rules.
I wondered who they were meant for exactly
    everyone or just people like us.

A SEAT AT THE TABLE

The secretary went over last month's minutes
brought up picketers at movie theaters and young people
protesting against Woolworth's in West Philly.
    How the club wrote letters to the managers about their
    hiring
practices and treating everyone fairly.
They discussed the housing crisis too. Teary-eyed
one of them mentioned a building that collapsed in the Seventh
Ward. "Remember that family?" the secretary asked.
Cousin spoke up. "Clergy, groups and clubs, politicians here on
Christian Street, have been raising Cain for years over the lack
of good, quality housing in the city."
"Finally, something is being done. A new housing project breaks
ground next year in North Philly. We have to keep up the
pressure. South Philly needs its fair share of good housing too."
They discussed other ways they could help our city and
community.
    Someone said their coffers were low, then mentioned
    holding a Christmas Extravaganza to raise funds for their
    group.

"We'll need an entertainer of note,"
    one of the briefcase ladies said.
"Someone the entire country knows.
    The right person could fill our coffers to bursting."

They threw out names.
Duke Ellington, for starters.
Langston Hughes was a friend of the New York woman's.
She'd call him, she said.
"Marian Anderson is a Philly girl
    always here visiting her mother,"

Cousin told them. "I could reach out to her."

At the end of their meeting
I stood up to sneak back to Lisa's room.
But someone spotted me.
Offered me a seat at the table.
Asked what I wished to be
    when I grew up.

"I'm not sure."

A woman wearing a hat shaped like a spaceship
took out a pen that looked like it was dipped in gold.
She wrote my name
at the top of a sheet of yellow paper
    with blue lines on it.

Dr. Hattie Mae Jenkins.

She pushed the paper to the next person.

Hattie Mae Jenkins, Business Owner,
    that lady wrote.

On it went
my name with different titles behind it
Lawyer
PhD
    I didn't know what that meant, but now I do.
LPN
Teacher
Engineer
Librarian
Author

Police Officer
Preacher
Mathematician
Mechanic
Homemaker.

"I never knew a woman could have so many jobs," I told them.

"One day
women will hold the exact same positions as men."
Cousin walked over to sit beside me.
   "Maybe even become president of the United States of
   America."

Someone wrote my name one last time.

Hattie Mae Jenkins
   Madame President.

PAYING SOMEBODY ELSE'S WAY

Later
I thought about those women
the way they spoke
the roads they took to get here.
    Adelaide and her mother
came top of mind.
She will *be* one of Cousin's girls
one day. I just know it.
She just needs a little help.

I swung my legs over the side of the bed.
    Got downstairs lick-e-ty-split.
Rumbled through kitchen closets.
"There you go." I took the Mason jar upstairs.
    Twisted open the lid
slid Cousin Abigail's dollar bills inside
along with spare change
    all I could find in pockets and drawers.
It wasn't much
    but a start.

ALL TOGETHER AGAIN

When the girls returned the next day
    it sounded like thunder rumbling
through the building.
Everybody was talking at the same time.
Opening and shutting doors.
Yelling how much they missed being there.
    "And you too, Miss Abigail . . ."
one of the girls said, holding on to Cousin
for dear life.

HATTIE'S HELPERS

We had a fine meal together
    went to our rooms
to put things away or do as we pleased.
Me
I pulled out my Mason jar.
Bert was in the closet
putting away a few new things.
"I smell glue.
What are you doing at your desk, Hattie?
Homework?"

"Something like that."

I took out a sheet of paper
wrote *Hattie's Helpers* on it in my finish handwriting
    glued it to the jar, smiling.
Mrs. Grable never said we couldn't
put ourselves on the volunteer list
by becoming philanthropists like Mrs. Wintergarden
starting our own organizations and clubs.
So I decided to start one of my own.

ADMITTING THE TRUTH

I ran downstairs to get
the latest copy of the *Tribune*.
Lisa followed me back upstairs, nearly tripping me.
    Halfway there
I turned around.
        Stamped my feet. "Quit it."

"Then tell me . . ." she yelled.

"Tell you what?"
    "You were in my room poking about
weren't you?"

I didn't answer.
    "My postcards.
The mailman said he handed them to you.
You put them on my dresser.
    Not Mr. Gage. Isn't that so?"
    I finally *had* to admit it.

"Who did you tell?"
"No one cares about your stupid mail."
She was talking about her room, I found out.
    "No one is permitted in it, ever."

I invaded her privacy, she told me
    promising to pay me back once and for all.

IN THE HOT SEAT

She told on me.

From the other side of the desk
Cousin Abigail asked me again
why I had violated Lisa's privacy.

I didn't have an answer.

"Lisa said someone had
been in her room, rummaging
through her things. I never would have suspected you
    though I guess I was foolish not to."

I apologized
hoped she wouldn't add
breaking and entering
to my list of crimes.

Cousin lifted a green glass pen
dipped it in an inkwell
scribbled something on a sheet of paper.
It took a while for her to look up at me.
"You are dismissed."

"Please don't make me leave.
I know I can improve
I just know it!"

"Cousin—"
It was the first time
    she called me that.

"We'll have no more talk of you leaving.
Apologize to Lisa.
And let us see if that will put an end to it."

THE TRICK THAT GOT PLAYED ON ME

Lisa met me in the hallway upstairs
and put her hand out.

"Give it to me."

"What?"
    "Give it to me."

"I don't have anything.
    I never took the letter."

"You read my father's letter?"

"No . . ."

"Then whose letter was it?"

I could kick myself. "Miss Abigail's."

Lisa went into her skirt pocket
and took out Gran's ring.
    "You will get it back over my dead body."

THE NEW OWNER OF GRAN'S RING

I followed her into her room.
She never liked the ring anyway, she said
 dropping it into a music box on her dresser.

"It's mine. I want it back."

What would Miss Abigail think about me
reading one of her letters? Lisa asked.
 "Besides, it's a postal violation
against the law to tamper with someone else's mail.
Get out. Now."

I stared at the music box.
Took a step or two.
 "It's my grandmother's. My great-grandmother's.
I still have the twine. The ring belongs on there."

Then I ought to have thought more carefully
before I put it in jeopardy, she said on her way to the door.
 Opening it, she pointed to the hallway
and invited me to leave.

GIRLS LIKE US

I'm not like Lisa
    or girls like her.
I'm more like Adelaide
    the sidewalk girl.
Fresh from the South.
Wanting something different
not sure how to get it.
Tripping over this and that
    running into people wishing
we never came in the first place.
    But we ain't going nowhere
I told myself on my way to my room.
    Then I wrote Brother a letter.
Asking where he's been. Why his letters
have stopped coming.

I am hugging you, he wrote back.
Busy as a bee.
Do not fret over that girl or the others.
You are ten times taller.
Whip smart, besides.
I'll meet you among the stars tonight.

WHAT LISA WANTS
FROM ME NOW

Lisa walked into our room without being invited.
    "I need you, Hattie" is all she said.

Bert told her to leave. "Now."
    I got up and walked out with her.

Lisa's room was still a storm.
    Stepping over clothes
she told me she has maids at home.
Her father sent one here, but Cousin Abigail
    would not permit her to stay.
Lisa lifted her foot
kicked a blouse across the room
like it was a football. "Clean it up."

I looked around
but didn't say a word.

"If you do what I tell you to, I might return the ring.
    Otherwise, my father has agreed to meet
with the board and have you expelled
and Miss Abigail replaced."

I wanted to shove her but kept my hands to myself. "What did she ever do to you?"

"Playing favorites is against the rules.
You should have been expelled for breaking into my room."

I thought about home.

About all the cleaning I did here too.
What was another room? Or more trash to toss?
Especially if it meant keeping Cousin out of trouble.
I owed her.

A NEW MAID AT SCHOOL

Lisa stayed the whole time.
Sitting at her desk
she gave me orders, like I was the maid.
I was to put the dresses on hangers in a particular fashion.
Fold the sweaters just so
    lay them in drawers
separated by tissue paper.
Put away her pearls and purses.
    Put clothes in her closet
in order by color, pattern and size.

It took all afternoon.

WORKING MY FINGERS TO THE BONES

I went to my room
sat at my desk.
Closed my eyes
took to the roof back home with James Henry.
Flew across the universe.

A little later
I got back to business.
I did my homework.
Worked on my spelling and handwriting
    completed two extra-credit assignments
one that turned out to be six pages long.
When Bert got in,
my head was on my desk
    my eyes were shut
while I worked out math problems in my head.
"Wake up. It's time to eat."

"I just can't," I said.
    "I'm too tired."

"No."
    Lisa stayed on my heels.
Following me downstairs into the dining room.

"I told you no."

TRAPPED

"No."
    Ignoring me, Lisa stayed on my heels.
Following me downstairs into the dining room.
"I told you to leave me alone. I'm not your maid, you know."
    "If you don't . . . do what I want . . . whenever I say so . . ."
She whispered in my ear
so the other girls couldn't hear.
""I'll throw
your granny's ring into the Schuylkill.
And you know it."

I guess it wasn't such a big thing
I told myself.
    I could iron her dresses.
Any girl worth her salt in Seed County could.
    "Satin easily burns." She smirked. "Do be careful."

Instead of eating lunch, I went to the laundry room on the next floor.
Set up the ironing board
    slid the dress over it.
Plugged in the iron. Once it got hot
I licked my finger and touched it to it.
When your spit sizzles
you know it's the right temperature.

On purpose
I scorched the inside hem of her gown.

FRIENDS TO THE END

I'd taken to moping on the front steps.
Complaining about Lisa whenever I could.

"Here."
Alabaster jumped off his bike
walked up to me, stuck his arm out.
"Ma sent these.
She hopes they make you feel better."

There they were
Gran's biscuits, sitting
in the bottom of a brown paper bag
    soaked in butter.

I turned my legs into a desk
reached into the bag.
"How'd she know they're the kind
my Gran makes?"

"Me and Mom know lots of things."

I broke the biscuit in two.
    Crumbs flew like pollen.
Alabaster said no
when I offered him some.
    "Ma makes 'em practically every night."

WHAT MA SUSPECTS ABOUT ME

Passing Bert on her bed
I hurried over to my desk.
Opened the drawer.
Pulled out a letter opener
read Ma's letter.
    I can tell something's not right, Ma wrote.
But Abigail says you're adjusting just fine.
Is it true?

I used writing paper
Bert's aunt shipped to her from New Orleans
the pen and inkwell
Brother sent me when I first came.

I love it here, I wrote back.
See you at Thanksgiving.

Out of nowhere, Bert
asked about my necklace.
She hadn't seen it lately, she said.

I lied. "It's old-fashioned
    out of date. I don't wear it anymore."
"Oh, Hattie Mae," she said. "How awful."

DECISIONS

A week later, Lisa's room was back the way it had been
    clothes asunder.
It slipped out. "What in the world happened?"

She can never make a choice, she told me.
Sometimes it takes six outfit changes
before she can decide on the perfect look.
Ten pairs of shoes before she picks one.

Stepping around clothes like land mines
she said for me to pick them up this instant,
like it was me who made the mess.

She asked again. Yelling this time.
I looked in the mirror over her dresser
for my old self
but could not find her anywhere.

THE SADDEST GIRL IN SCHOOL

I stumped out the house.
Sat on the porch steps
with my fist holding my chin.

Alabaster and his bike were on the sidewalk
like a chariot ready to fly me away.
    "Hop on, Miss Hattie."

I stayed put
sitting on the top step in a wool sweater
and mittens
moping over my dilemma.

"Miss Hattie."

"Yes."

"What's it like to go to a school like yours?"

I'd tell him some other time, I said.
    "Couldn't be much fun."

"What makes you say that?"

"You.
I never seen a girl more solemn."

THE DAY I LEARNED TO RIDE A BIKE

To prove Alabaster wrong, I went over to his bike.
Leaning it sideways
    I hopped on.
He laughed.
My foot
slipped off the pedal too many times to count.
    Finally, I rode up to the telephone pole
two feet or so. A start.
I jumped off after a dog barking
rattled me.
Back on, I fell off for no good reason.

Alabaster finally came over.
Holding the bike by the seat to steady it
he encouraged me to keep at it.
    "I been wondering when
you would learn that some things you got to take into your own hands."

BY AND BY

After my lesson
I went on a long, long walk
    smiling and happy.
I ended up at the theater
wishing for popcorn
and a seat inside.
But I stayed put
watching the picketers
    five in total.
Bert nowhere to be found.

Do they ever get tired?
I wondered.
    I was tired of cleaning up
and scrubbing after Lisa.
Holding on to secrets of one kind or another.
Of feeling like I hadn't earned the right to be at
Cousin's school.

A man walked up to one of the women and stopped.
"Is it doing any good?"

"We'll know by and by.
But if we quit, we'll never find out."

She smiled.
He tipped his hat and went on his way.

Is it doing any good
me attending Cousin's school
trying to climb a ladder some

think is only meant for them.
Guess
I'll know by and by.

PROUD HERITAGE

It's no wonder Lisa and the rest
walk with their heads high up.
Think they're the cat's meow,
I thought to myself in class
    after an hour discussing
contributions so many here made to the city.
    They come from good stock
brave people
who never stopped
even when folks said to be satisfied with their lot.

I raised my hand.
Stood at attention.
    "One day I plan to add to Philadelphia's history
leave my mark on the city."

"That is what we like to hear, Hattie Mae.
Our young women
following in the shoes of Charlotte Forten Grimké
and Mary Ann Shadd Cary
suffragists and abolitionists
journalists and teachers
enslaved and free, resilient every step of the way
taking their rightful place at the seat of power
not asking permission to change the world."

Lisa sat up taller.
    I took out a pencil
wrote myself a short note.

Hattie Mae Jenkins, President of
Hattie's Helpers

TK

STANDING ON MY OWN TWO FEET

PAGE SIX

Dinner and chores done
I rushed to my room
kicked off my shoes
threw 'em under my bed
and laid belly down on the floor
reading the society pages.
    It'd been a while since I had.

I checked for my name
because of something I might have done
but wasn't aware of yet.

I was glad to see
the paper had other things to talk about
like families in town visiting relations for the holidays
the Bruces and the Browns
Mr. Nicolson and his new bride
Barbara Anne Jones, beauty queen at Mount Vernon College
entertainers
clubs holding jitterbug contests for prizes
charity events
an update on Douglass Hospital
there is talk of them merging
with Mercy Hospital School of Nursing.
Regardless
I knew if I wasn't careful
Lisa would make certain
    my name ended up on page six.
But never in a good way.

TAKING BACK WHAT
RIGHTFULLY BELONGS TO ME

At lunch
I took myself upstairs to change my shoes
so I said.
But that wasn't the truth.

Holding my breath
I opened Lisa's door and went into her room
closed the door behind me, quick.

Her clothes were where
they were supposed to be
in closets and drawers, thanks to me.
    Her shoes were on a rack by the wall
in rows and pairs. I was proud of myself.

"Quiet," I said when I opened the music box.

Smiling, I reached inside
for what belonged to my family.
Only, Gran's ring wasn't there.

Nervous, I ran to her bed
pulled back the covers
looked in her dresser drawer
throwing clothes every which way.
    I went to her closet
and checked every single one of her pockets.

Didn't find Gran's ring anywhere.

"Hattie Mae!"
It was Cousin Abigail.
"What on earth are you doing in Lisa's room? And for the second time. Get. To. My. Office. Now!"

BEING PUNISHED AGAIN

Cousin scolded me
forbade me
from going on the next three outings:
an opera put on by college students at Mother Bethel
a visit to Douglass Hospital to hand out bags of candies to the
youngest patients
a ballet performed by the Ballet Russe de Monte Carlo at the
Academy of Music
     which I wasn't sure I wanted to go to anyway
     because Negroes are given the worst seats
     even though Colored dancers perform on stage with the
     white ones.

"While your classmates have fun," Cousin told me,
"you shall be at school, writing on the blackboard
over and over again
     in cursive, by the way,
I will keep my hands to myself."

My penmanship would also be graded.

I raised my hand.
"What about Lisa?"
I mentioned her
     because she never gets in trouble
and still had Gran's ring.

Cousin said she was doing her best to be fair.
"But Lisa had no part in this. Besides
her father contributes a great deal
to our schools' bottom line.
"You attend—"

I finished her sentence.
"For free."

She sat in the chair beside me.
"You are not a charity case.
We are family . . ."
　　She lowered her voice. Lifted my chin.
　　"But everything isn't as it seems, Hattie Mae.
Not with Lisa nor with you or me.
Just know I am doing my best . . . I truly am."

BERT'S DREAMS OF BEING ON THE SILVER SCREEN

Bert sat at her desk, cutting up last week's *Tribune*.
Gluing her favorite actors onto notebook paper.
"I went to the movies."
    I flopped down on my bed.
"Were they picketing?"

She didn't answer.
"Sometimes I look up at the marquee
and see my name up there in lights."

One of the churches was putting on a play, I had heard.
"You ought to try out for it," I told her.

Bert got to her feet
still holding scissors on her way over to me.

"My father thinks cultured girls
are above acting and dancing on stage
    working the chitlin circuit
wearing shiny tight things
    feathers and skimpy dresses."

She shimmied over to me
hopped around doing the jitterbug. I joined in.
Out of breath, she told me she'll live in Paris one day.
Dance with Josephine Baker.
Write poems sitting at a Parisian café next to Langston Hughes.
Interview Paul Robeson.

All of a sudden she looked scared.

"What if my dreams never come true?"

"They will. Mine too.
They have to."

A LONG STROLL ON A COLD FALL NIGHT

The second week in November
was breezy and wet.
But we went for a stroll nonetheless.
We shared an umbrella, Bert and me.
Shivered
in our wool coats, mittens and hats.

Bert stopped at a store window with a sign in it.
Girls' High is putting on a Christmas play.
She said she wished she could be in it.
"If I am going to be famous.
    I have to start practicing now."

"You don't have nearly as far to climb as I do.
Why, I bet
your uncle would say you have what it takes already."

Her face lit up.
"He has plenty of times."
    Her uncle is a musician.
Bert's family stopped speaking to him
after he dropped out of Harvard to take up the horn
    and married a woman with no pedigree.

"Once he introduced me to Count Basie
who patted me on the head and said,
'Hang in there, kiddo,' after listening to me sing."

I suppose no matter
where you are on the ladder
everyone wants to climb a little higher.

LIGHTS, CAMERA, ACTION

I took her by the arm
started walking faster this time.

"Pretend you're somebody else."
I looked her way.
"An actress from your favorite movie."

Bert looked around.
"Out here? Oh, I couldn't."

Later that night
right in front of my eyes
Bert turned into somebody else.
    And a light bulb went off in my head.
That's why she copies other people.
She's practicing.
Rehearsing.
Not cheating or scared to be herself.

Sitting up
I pretended to munch on popcorn
while I watched her put on a show
turning into Lisa, Eiffel Tower, then the actress Bette Davis
    singing and dancing and acting in whispers.

A hour later she made another confession.
"Sometimes when I go missing . . . Oh, never mind."

"Bert, you can trust me. Honest."

To convince her
I told her about Lisa.

Me cleaning her room sometimes twice a week.

Finally she spit out the truth.

"I go to the movies and protest. Not that I can talk about it.
It is not the kind of thing my father and his family approve of.
My mother's people are different. 'Those who have been blessed with plenty
must give plenty back to the world in return,' they believe."
Bert told me later that she had other reasons for protesting too.
"When I become a star, I want everybody everywhere to come see me in the movies."

OLD PHILADELPHIA

Bert talked and talked about her family coming to Philadelphia in 1867
>but not empty-handed. They bought barns and banks and buildings to rent

she said, gave their daughters and sons the same opportunities. Hobnobbing with high society was always at the top of their list, she said laughing.
She brought up the sorts of people her parents hung around with, but only because
I pushed her.

>"The Trowers and the Baptests

the Mossell family of course. The Dorseys, the Fausets and Duvelles."

>"All snobs most likely," I said, thinking about Lisa and her father.

"Not most," Bert told me. "My mother likes fine things, good food, traveling and people who do good in the world, she likes to say."

>Undoing my robe, I got under my covers. "Bert, what's it like to live in a mansion?"

It's all she's ever known, she told me. "So it's like any other house, I suppose."

>Why didn't she ever invite me to stay over or visit her there? I asked.

>"I find that it changes people or the way they see me. And I would

much rather you accept me the way I am. Is that okay?"

>I said it was and I meant it.

STANDING MY GROUND

Lisa came into our room early in the morning
> while we were still barefooted
and only dressed in our slips.
"I spilled tea on my sheets."
> She pranced over to me.
"They need to be changed, instantly."

She sounded so ridiculous, Bert laughed.

I ignored her
went about my business
opening drawers, taking out socks.

"As you know, sheets need to be ironed.
You might want to get started now."

In my head I counted to ten.
Then told her I wasn't permitted
to go into her room ever again.
"Miss Abigail forbids it."

She stomped her foot.
Bert laughed. I told Lisa
if she had a problem with it
she could take it up with Miss Abigail.
Then I pointed to the door. "Now go!
You are disturbing us."
She marched out the room
> without saying a mumbling word.

NEW DIGS

Finally, I got around to taking the volunteer list to Mrs. Grable.
    There were eleven places
the girls said they wanted to volunteer at.
Three hospitals.
A nursing home.
Five churches.
Two doctor's offices.
Most in our community.

Mrs. Grable posted the list
in her classroom.
After school I went to my suitcase to get a few things.
I sat on the floor with a pair of scissors
a spool of thread
and a tin of needles.
    Gran calls them essentials
for any girl worth her salt.

Bert came in later asking what I was up to.
"Nothing."
I retreated to the closet
closed the door behind me.
It took me hours
long after dark
to shorten sleeves on a dress or two
sew lace onto the collars
hem the skirts once I'd cut off an inch or so.

The next morning
in the spare room, I set the ironing board up.
Pressed out the wrinkles.

Soon as I folded them nice and neat
two girls came in. Asked what I was up to.

I didn't say.

A SHORT VISIT WITH ADELAIDE

I felt like skipping across the street.
    Doing cartwheels.
But I was one of Miss Abigail's girls
so I took my time
rang the bell once, even though
it took forever for someone to answer.

A man opened the door.
I introduced myself.
Mentioned the name of our school
and why I was there.
"May I speak with Miss Adelaide?"
    He scratched his head and smiled.
"I think I can find her for you."

She and her mother came to the door.
    I handed Adelaide the package
and explained things.
The school wants us to volunteer
for organizations in the neighborhood.
    "I decided to be my own organization.
See." I showed her the homemade card.
"Hattie's Helpers. That's me."

While she opened the package
I explained how this was not charity.
That I was just being neighborly
    like folks do back home.

Adelaide put her hand up to my ear
so only I could hear.

"At night I imagine I attend your school.
And I am dressed as well as any girl."

Her mother shook my hand
said a businesswoman deserves respect.
　"I'm not a businesswoman."
"Your business card says different," Mrs. Carolyn said.
　"Soon you'll be hiring, I imagine.
Count us in if you need any help."

STANDING ON BUSINESS

At lunch
I took myself upstairs to change
into my red shoes.
A businesswoman needs to
stand out from regular folk,
Alabaster told me.
    I am done with punishments, though
so I plan to tell Cousin after my last class
of the day
why I am not wearing my white
saddle shoes.
I hope she understands.

MORE BAD NEWS FOR LISA

My shoes were dull
so in honor of Alabaster
I buffed and polished 'em.
Which is why I was late to class.
Which is why Mrs. Grable sent me to the office.
But somebody was already there with Cousin.
Lisa.
I could see her through the crack in the door.
But I only heard a word or two of what was said:
    father
          Thanksgiving
canceled.

THE ONE QUESTION I COULDN'T ANSWER

Someone closed Cousin Abigail's door.
    I got out of there quick
ended up in the bathroom up the hall.
A little while later Lisa was standing
at the sink next to me.

She didn't say a word.
    That never happens.

I didn't open my mouth
    make a sound
move a muscle.
    That never happens either.

Through the mirror I saw tears
    coming down her cheeks.
"Do you ever miss your family, Hattie?"

All the time, I told her.

"Do they miss you?
Ever?"
She looked at me through the mirror.
    "Your family has to. Don't you think?"

She never answered.

CHOICES, CHOICES

In our room that night
Bert and I try to answer the question
Lisa raised in the bathroom.
> Does your family have to love you?

What happens when they don't?

"But why would she ask you such a question, Hattie?
You are her enemy.
Not that you have earned it."
> Well, the holidays are coming.

Where will Lisa go,
if she can't go home? I wondered.
Some of the girls plan to join their families
in Martha's Vineyard
> the Pocono Mountains

Boston
> New York

California.
Eiffel Tower is going South.

The rest will stay in the city with family.
Me, Bert and a few others
> will stay at school.

In a postcard last week
Daddy gave me a choice.
Come home for Thanksgiving or Christmas.
They could not afford both.
> We are getting a new house.

They are saving money for the down payment.

WHAT DOROTHY'S MOTHER TOLD HER

Right before church
Lisa passed me in the hall upstairs
    making sure not to look my way.
But I heard
what Dorothy said a few hours ago.
"Come home with me for Thanksgiving, Lisa.
My mother says an extra plate on the table
is no bother."

"I have family. But I would rather stay here
    and attend to my studies.
Which is why I am light-years ahead
of the rest of you academically."

Into her room Lisa went
closing the door quietly.
Dorothy looked my way.
    "My mother says it is a disgrace
the way her parents treat her."

A QUESTION FOR PASTOR

We gathered at Mother Bethel
and gave thanks. Most of us anyhow.
Lisa attends St. Peter Claver Catholic Church all by herself.
Of course Mr. Gage drives her
    which makes him late for services with us every week.
On my knees at the bench
    I had a little talk with God.
And asked him to go easy on people
who didn't have much.
    And make Lisa not be so mean.

By the time the pastor preached
Cousin had to elbow me to keep me awake.

After service
pastor shook hands
with the congregation.
Finally it was my turn.

"How are you this fine
getting-up morning, young lady?"

"Good, thank you."
    Then I asked him a question.
"Do people have to love you?"

He said no, but it sure makes
life easier if they do.
    "Maybe mean people
are too hard to love, and that's why
nobody likes them," I told him.
    "Maybe mean people

need more love than the rest of us."
He winked. Took my hand
and prayed for Lisa—
even though I never said her name.

HAPPY THANKSGIVING

The day before Thanksgiving
we went to the YMCA on Christian
served meals to men down on their luck
some passing through town
    others new to the city with no family to speak of.

We stood behind tables
watched them file in
nodding at us in our aprons and hairnets.

I was in between Cousin and a woman from her social club.
Lisa was beside a boy and another grown-up.
Holding serving spoons and forks
we watched the men line up
quiet
smiling
thankful
holding their hats in their hands.

I scooped up stewed cranberries
put them on plates
along with ham slices baked in pineapples.
    I said, "Happy Thanksgiving"
a hundred times, I'd say.

Bert was responsible
for forking over two slices of turkey per man
pouring on the gravy with giblets.
Lisa pouted
but joined in at Cousin's insistence
adding dressing
and cornbread muffins to their plates.

The others took care of the rest, including
macaroni and cheese, potatoes au gratin
chicken
    fried, baked, boiled
collards, of course.

THANKFUL

    We were done serving
    when one of the girls said
we should sing while the men ate dessert.

Ella ran to the piano
a black Steinway
that looked as beat-up as some of the men.
    Bert sat beside her on the bench
facing the audience.
Eyes closed, she belted out the words to "Happy Days Are Here Again."
    The men joined in.
    The rest of us too.

I was thankful.

TEARS FOR LISA

On the way home
walking under streetlamps
our toes cold as ice
Bert admitted how much she
missed her family.

I shoved my hands in my coat pocket.
"Why didn't you go home?"

She made snowballs.
Threw them up the street.
    "My parents travel to Africa every Thanksgiving
to do missionary work." Her sister attends a boarding school
in Connecticut;
Canterbury Female Boarding School for Colored girls, she told
us.
"I stay here. She stays there."

Once Gran said
folks who came North lost some things.
"Family ties mostly."

WATCHING FAMILIES CELEBRATE TOGETHER

Christian Street was all lit up
window drapes pushed back
families at tables, passing plates
eating
    some in chairs, some standing.

Folks got out of cars
smiling and laughing
carrying platters and dishes covered in foil.
Holding the little ones' hands.
Talking loud
noisy.
    I thought about Gran and what she said.
Plenty folk up North
holding tight to what they came with.
Family mostly.

UNWELCOME

The day after Thanksgiving
Lisa's mood turned extra sour.

"Maybe your father will be home by Christmas, Lisa."
I was being nice, I thought.

She set fire to me with her tongue.
But it's not true what she said
that I'm as country as cotton
    unsophisticated.
        Ill prepared for a large city like Philadelphia.

I shot back, "Well, at least I'm not mean and spiteful."
"A thief besides." I was thinking about Gran's ring.
    Lucky for her my hands aren't like they used to be
changing into fists quick and in a hurry.
They stayed by my side
    limp as slimy
old fish.
Lisa turned on her heel
to go speak with Cousin about girls like me.

SPENDING THE DAY WITH A TRUE-BLUE FRIEND

Days later, Alabaster followed me like a shadow
from the sidewalk to the back of the house
where the trash was.
He wanted me to go to the shoe shop with him.

I shook my head no.
    "I have work to do, Alabaster,"
I said, watching my breath fog up the air.

I bent down beside the trash can.
Picked up what the alley cats didn't finish
    bits and pieces of last night's supper.
Alabaster helped.

"Once you're done
you'll come with me, right?"

"Do I get to ride the bike, at least?"

"I wiped it down just for you."

VISITING ALABASTER'S MOTHER'S SHOE SHOP

This time I was no better on the bike
but no worse either.
He trotted along.
I wobbled my way to his mother's shop
up one block and down the next.

Alabaster let me go
in the shoe shop ahead of him.

He turned on the lights.
One overhead with a string for pulling
and a beautiful lamp on the table in the corner
near the sewing machine.

Shoes everywhere
sat in rows and rows of cubbyholes on the wall
some alone
some with company
others stuck together with thick rubber bands.
Yellow notes inside 'em told owners
what was done
and what money was due, Alabaster said.

They were all sorts of colors
    black and green
gray and yellow
    red and white
and everything in between.

"Where's your ma?"
    "I never said she was here, did I?"
She was volunteering near the docks

serving soup to the poor, he said.
"She'll be here later."

I joined Alabaster by the window
    near the sewing machine.

"Some shoes need gluing
some resoling.
I can do it all."
Holding on to his suspenders, he looked proud of himself.

If customers don't pay
or pay and forget to pick up their shoes or boots
they end up on his feet
    or his brother's or mother's
    or get donated to churches in the area.

I stared at my feet.
At the shoes Alabaster gave me.
Feels like they have wings
    when I'm with him.

"Miss Hattie."

"Yes."

"I'm starting to feel sorry for her."

I knew who he meant.

"Seems like nobody wants her."
He started up the machine.
    "Y'all at school might be all the family she got."

"No, Cou—Miss Abigail says
her father is on the board.
He's occupied with work, that's all."

"What if she's mean because she doesn't *feel* wanted.
Like an old hound dog left to his own devices."
He put his foot down on the pedal of the sewing machine.

I watched the needle go up and down in a hurry
stitching the sole to the shoe.

It wasn't easy, I could tell.
He had to start and stop a lot.
Make sure the needle that went into the shoe
made nice, even stitches.

While he worked, I thought about Dog
a shepherd in Seed County
with no home to go to
but plenty of people to love him
feed him
rub him
play catch with him.
He was gentle and kind
    sweet as molasses.
Not like other dogs
with no one to care for them
who would chase you home
nipping at your heels the whole time—
like Lisa.

ALABASTER'S GOOD IDEA

"It's odd, Hattie, don't you think
for a person not to have
one single
    relative or family friend to check in on 'em?"

It never crossed my mind.
    But heading home
I chewed on it.
I thought about what Alabaster and the pastor said.
Cousin's letter too.
Maybe I didn't know everything.
    But Cousin Abigail would.
Once I got back I asked her if Lisa had relatives here.
She told me it was Lisa's private business
and not my concern.

She was filing at the time.
Setting aside a stack of folders.
    That's when I got the idea.

A MIDNIGHT RIDE TO THE FIRST FLOOR

I didn't go to sleep.
If I had
I might not have woken up
in time to sneak into
Cousin's file cabinet.

It was easy getting out of my room
with Bert gone for the weekend.
Sneaking up the hall was a breeze too.
I know where the squeaks in the floor are
and how to avoid them.

Girls
snored in their rooms
like they were in a band
each playing a different instrument.

I stopped at the top of the stairs.
Decided to take the railing
so the steps wouldn't rat on me.

Lying on the banister
belly down
I held on tight
pushed off
went
sliding fast and quick
taking every twist and turn the banister took
     almost falling off it at the end of the ride.

My heart beat like a drum.
My palms sweated.

But I kept going
    tiptoeing sometimes
stopping in my tracks a time or two.
I felt like a thief letting myself in her office.
Not that it stopped me from turning on the light
shutting the door behind me.

SPYING ON LISA

I got to Bert's file first
    opened it up
then put it back. It just didn't seem right
to spy on a good friend.

Lisa's file was thicker than all the rest
not that I was surprised.
I looked at her grade reports
    notes from teachers complaining
about her behavior.
Pictures of her family. The three of them.
    Her stepmother never smiled, I noticed.

Ten words on an envelope caught my eye.

CONFIDENTIAL
    PRIVATE
PERSONAL
    DO NOT SHARE WITH ANYONE, ANYTIME EVER.

I had to open it.

WHAT I LEARNED ABOUT LISA'S FATHER

Dear Miss Abigail,
My wife and I have gotten a divorce.
It is cowardice of me, I know, but I cannot face
my daughter and share the news. And her stepmother
has no desire to.
This information cannot get out under any circumstances.
My position as the president
of one of the largest hospitals north of the Mason-Dixon Line
is nearly secured. They do not hire divorcés or single fathers.
As you can see, my hands are tied.
Please accept my thanks and appreciation for your discretion
and caring for Lisa. I know when she is unsettled and afraid
she can be intolerable. But what choice do I have
but to depend on you and your outstanding school?
I am the only child of an only child who only has one child.
Your school has been a haven for the both of us.

Yours truly,
Dr. Jerome Connolly
Surgeon, Professor,
Doctor of Neurology

Cousin wrote back to him many times
suggesting that he visit Lisa, if only for a short while.
 "She knows something is wrong. And has turned into a
 tyrant.
I fear her behavior is simply her way of striking out at a world
she believes is being woefully unfair to her."

SHARING SECRETS WITH MY ROOMMATE

I told Bert about Lisa.
I had to tell someone.
    We were so afraid
she might hear us that we
pulled the covers over our heads
when we talked about her
even though our door was closed.
    "Divorce? But, he's Catholic.
Your parents cannot go to confession or Catholic church if they divorce,"
Bert said. "And what about Lisa; Communion and confession?
It's all just terrible."

PATCHES AND SCHOLARSHIPS

They were on the sidewalk again.
Shivering
imagining too,
her mom said when I got to them.

"Here." She handed me a box.
"Our contribution."

It had labels in it
white fabric
in the shapes of kidney beans.
Hattie's Helpers, they said.
     The letters were all stitched in red.

I hugged 'em both
ran into the house and came back with my Mason jar.
"In September
you will get the first scholarship. I promise."

CLASS TRIP: A DAY AT THE MUSEUM

It's never too cold out
to learn something new about the world
or to elevate oneself, Cousin Abigail told us
on our way to the museum.

Of course we walked.
It's the best way to advertise the school, she thinks.
Dressed smartly in our uniforms
with matching coats and rubbers
we walked like ducks in a long, straight row
over sidewalks made of bricks
     and streets that went on for blocks.

Not long after we started
we caught sight of an old man
with a straw hat on his head
     and a thin black scarf underneath it.
Lisa laughed.
Said she could smell him.

I told him to have a good day.

Like always, Eiffel Tower
tried her best to impress Lisa.
Laughing
she pointed out the women
who do day's work
some standing on corners
waiting to be picked up by women
who drive them to fancy neighborhoods
     to sweep and mop

wash and iron, dust and cook.
    Gran used to do such work.

"My father believes one has to pull
one's own self up by the bootstraps,"
Eiffel Tower said.
"He did. My grandfather as well.
People are lazy, you know."

LEARNING TO MIND MY OWN BUSINESS

I held my tongue
not that it was easy.
A bit later
I noticed Lisa lagging behind the rest of us.
When Dorothy mentioned it to her
Lisa said,
"Stuff a sock in your mouth.
    And leave me alone."
I walked away.

BACK TO THE FARM

At the museum
we went from room to room
learned about different
artists.
Different styles of painting
baroque
abstract
contemporary
impressionist
how the French liked to paint outdoors in the 1800s.
The way light and colors change depending on what your eyes
focus on
and the lighting in the room.

We learned so much
listened so hard
took so many notes
    my head started spinning.

What I liked best
was the watercolors
people boating or
strolling through grass, carrying umbrellas
    even without a hint of rain.

For a minute
    I pretended to be one of them.
It's how I accidentally stepped
on Lisa's new boot
    flown in from Paris.
    A gift from her father.

The next thing I knew she was
shoving me
hard
telling me to go back to the farm.

ONE OF MISS ABIGAIL'S GIRLS

I thought about what Pastor said
and ignored her.
Took myself to another room.
Ran into Adelaide.
It was her mother's day off.

"You should meet the other girls."
	I got permission before
I took her by the hand.

They remembered seeing her.
Some shook her hand.
Bert took a pretty pink fuzzy scarf from around her neck
	and tied it on Adelaide.
"Miss Abigail's girls always look elegant,"
she told her.

Right then Lisa showed up.
Laughing, she repeated to Adelaide
what she told me once
that she was as country as cotton
	unsophisticated as I was
ill prepared for a large city like Philadelphia.
It was her fault that Adelaide was crying.

GIVING LISA HER DUE

I hit her.
    I had to.
Good and hard.
She had it coming.
    It was long overdue.
Just like Titus, who teased Brother to no end
just because he knew he could.

THE THINKER

Lisa cried and
went running to find Cousin
who was near a giant statue of a man
sitting down
leaning his chin on his fist
like he was thinking.

KICKED OUT

She hollered at me.
    I yelled back
even louder.
Cousin tried to quiet us both
    but it didn't work.

A guard showed up and said we had to leave. "Now."
He escorted us out the museum.
Told Cousin,
"Do not return until you civilize them."

She gave him a piece of her mind
    chastising him like he was a child
with her finger in his face.
    "Come, ladies," she said once she was done.
"This gentleman has no idea who he is speaking with.
The entire museum board and the president
shall hear from me posthaste.
    I know every single one of them."

SHUT UP, LISA

Outside
still rattled
Cousin Abigail told us she had never been
so embarrassed or insulted.

Lisa raised her hand
asked if it wasn't true that country girls
were just boys in disguise.
"Rough as cowhands.
As civilized as mules.
Riffraff."

"Silence, Lisa!
I have had enough
      of you for a lifetime!" Cousin Abigail said.
I nearly clapped.

IN TROUBLE AGAIN

The next day
Cousin interrupted Mrs. Britain's class.
It was me she wanted.

"Come along, Hattie.
There's business we need to attend to."
Cousin sounded disappointed.

"What about Lisa?"
    "I will deal with her later."

By the time we left the room
my mind was made up.
    I didn't want to be one of Cousin's girls anymore.

A BRIGHT AND SHINING STAR

It took a while
for the corner store owner in Detroit
to give Ma the message that Cousin needed to speak with her.
And for Ma to get to the back of the store
opposite the soda fountain, where the phone booth is.

Cousin spoke low
and quiet
when she asked Ma how she was doing
then told her what good weather
we were having for the first week of December.

Soon
she got to the heart of the matter.
"I think Hattie Mae is having difficulty adjusting."
She added
how much she had tried to refrain from making this call.
    I tried to be a big girl and not cry.

Under her breath, Cousin Abigail said,
    "She willfully breaks the rules.
Takes liberties when I am otherwise engaged.
Does not get along with the other girls
as well as she should. The list goes on."

Ma was as quiet as a clogged pipe.

Cousin surprised me by saying,
    "Perhaps this was all a mistake."

That's when Ma spoke up.
"If she's not doing her best, it's for a reason.

Something or somebody at *your* school is
a thorn in her shoe."
Ma lowered her voice and asked who it was.

All the tears I'd kept inside since coming here
came out.
Snot too.
Ma told me I am loved
perfect in her eyes.
"Now, pull yourself together, child."

I stood up tall
blowing my nose into a handkerchief
supplied by Cousin Abigail.

"Remember who you are, Hattie Mae."

Before she got off the phone
Ma told me to watch for the mail.
And keep my chin up.

"Yes, Ma."

"Everything will be all right.
    Do you hear me?"

"I hear you, Ma."

"And, Abigail," she said,
"do not give up on her.
One day Hattie's star will shine
ten times brighter than each of ours."

A CHICKEN ON THE PORCH

I went hunting for Alabaster
because he's somebody you can talk to about hard things.

His ma's shoe store was closed
but I found him close by.
Would it be so bad if I did stay?
    he wanted to know
holding out his bike
like he wanted me to take a spin.
I shook my head no.
He sat on the steps of the house
next to his.
    "I'd miss you a mighty lot if you did go."

"I don't belong here. Cousin knows.
And she's never been fair to me.
    I see that now."

He flapped his arms.
"You plain chicken, ain't ya?
Scared maybe those girls are right
    about your status?"

"I'm done talking, Alabaster."
I looked away.

Surprising me
Alabaster told me to go home.
"Only chickens we need here in Philadelphia
are the ones at the grocery store
waiting to be plucked and served for supper."

"I am not chicken!"
    I rose up quick.

"Then prove it." He stood up.
"Stay."

I ignored him.
stomped the ground hard
like grapes were under my feet.
    Then I took myself back to school.

WHAT MA SENT

It was like Ma sent it on a rocket ship
had birds deliver it
her package got to me so quick.

She addressed it to
    Mademoiselle Hattie Mae of Philadelphia, Pa
Station D.

I sat on my bed to open it.
Ma hadn't changed all the way, I saw.
    Two sentences were all she wrote.

"Arriving in two days. Need to see for myself
how my Hattie Mae is doing."

PENNSYLVANIA STATION

Ma left the train station
carrying one small brown suitcase
and a chocolate cake in a carrying case.
    Peeking past her
I searched for Brother and Daddy.

"They wanted to come," she told me.
"But this time is for girls only.
Do you mind?"

I minded.
But never said so.

Wearing a thin gray dress
    covered with blue butterflies
and a tweed coat better suited for summer
Ma didn't seem bothered
by the chill in the air
or snow flurries dancing around us.
Smiling
she hugged me for the first time in months.

I
cried so hard I shook.

"It's okay."
Ma pulled my hat down over my ears.
"Every problem can be licked."

A BRAND-NEW JAMES HENRY

I introduced Ma to Mr. Gage
who took her suitcase
put it in the trunk
and drove us home.

Along the way
Ma brought up James Henry.
Asked if I missed him.

I missed him terribly sometimes
like now
like yesterday
and the day before
like last week too.
Half a person
that's how a twin feels when their twin
is far away.

Ma said James Henry barely
frets or shakes
now
that she's back on her feet.

He even has his own telescope.
Purchased brand-new
    with money earned from collecting cans
    sweeping up leaves
shoveling snow.

Hearing such good news
    should have made me feel better.

It didn't.
James Henry was moving on.
I was the one who was stuck now.

ON OUR BEST BEHAVIOR

The girls met Ma at the door
with hellos
    and welcome.

Lisa kindly took her coat
    hung it in the closet.
But not of her own accord.
We each had our assignments.

Mr. Gage walked Ma's suitcase upstairs.
Cousin Abigail took the cake
after chatting with us awhile in the parlor.
She said that Ma
could go upstairs to rest
before lunch if she wanted.

Ma was all smiles.
But stayed where she was.
"May I have a bit of time with my Hattie?"
She pulled me close. Of course Cousin approved.

A LUNCH FIT FOR ROYALTY

Bert met us in the dining room.
Said hello
escorted Ma and me to the table.
    Cousin Abigail's rules.

Handwritten name cards
sat beside china plates trimmed in gold
    so each of us knew where our seats were.
Me and Ma next to one another.
Bert across from Cousin.

QUEEN FOR A DAY

We each did our part
to make Ma's lunch a success
 even those not invited.

This morning
Eiffel Tower and Margaret
polished the silverware.
Upstairs
in the sewing room
I starched
and ironed cloth napkins stiff
 all six made by hand
 ours.
I folded them neatly
set 'em on a white linen tablecloth
next to the plates.
Complaining
Lisa set teacups on saucers
meant for coffee. None for us girls
 Cousin is fond of saying.

Margaret put out the silverware.

Ma walked in the room
stopped in her tracks.
 "Oh my, I feel like a queen."

"You are, Cousin—"
 Cousin Abigail's mouth shut
faster than a rabbit trap.

Bert had questions
I could tell.
Her eyes stayed on me all through lunch.

MAKING UP MY MIND

Salad
sourdough bread
pepper pot stew and baked pheasant
filled our bellies full.
But everyone has room
for Gran's five-layer chocolate cake
and Bert's Dutch apple pie.
    Cousin did the slicing.
Bert insisted on passing it around.

Sipping coffee, Cousin asked Ma
what Daddy's thoughts were about school and me.

"He thinks she should come home."

"And you?"
    Ma said she's on the fence about things.

Cousin reached for the creamer
poured some in her cup and
    looked up at me. "And what are your thoughts, Hattie?"

Gran's words came back to me.
    Ain't no harm in admitting
that something don't suit or fit you
the way you expected.
With my head high
I told Cousin, "I think it's best
that I leave when Ma does."

LISTENING TO OTHER PEOPLE'S OPINIONS

"Then come home," Ma said.

Bert looked disappointed.
"Alabaster was sure you would stay."

"I never promised him I would."

"He was hoping.
    Me too."

Bert's hand found mine and held on.
"School would be awful without you,"
she whispered.

"Boarding schools often assist children
with discovering themselves and their purpose.
Maybe she was always too young," Cousin Abigail said.

Ma added steaming-hot coffee to her cup.
Said whatever I wanted to do was fine with them.
"As long as it's your decision."

LET THEM EAT PIE

We heard a knock at the front door.
It was Alabaster.
I could see him through the glass
so I jumped up to answer.

He was delivering shoes, he said
when he saw me and Ma headed up the street
about an hour or so ago.

"She can't meet you just now."
I looked back in the house.
Saw Cousin seated next to Ma
talking
looking more serious than before.

"Yesterday Bert promised if I stopped by
she would see to it I got pie—
one slice for me plus one for Ma.
Yesterday was her birthday.
She said she didn't want no cake
that we needed our flour
for more important things.
    I do not agree.
But that's how Ma is.

Bert came to the door.
    Said Cousin sent her to bring me back.
Looking at Alabaster peculiar-like she said,
"Did you hear?
Hattie's leaving school for good."
    "That isn't true."
I stepped onto the front porch.

"See, you are chicken."
He flapped his arms like wings.

I stomped my feet in protest. "Take that back," I yelled.

He didn't. And he wouldn't, he said
looking cross for the first time since we'd met.

RESTLESS

Ma and I slept in a spare bed
up the hall
side by side
but she hardly got a wink of sleep
with all the tossing I did.

It was Alabaster's words that done it.
They stuck to me
like
soles on shoes
salt on pork
ink on parchment paper.

Chicken.
Maybe I was
in more ways than he knew.

A QUIET BREAKFAST WITH MA

Cousin and the girls were at church.
I would have been too, normally.
We girls get no choice here.
Ma is different.
Once she was done snoring the night away
she made me a good hearty breakfast
    oats with strawberries
    fatback bacon cured in a smokehouse miles off
    eggs from hens in Jersey
    thick
    homemade bread Ma brought along with her.
It was good to have her all to myself.

THINGS THAT HAPPENED LONG AGO

Outside
under a bright sun
I half expected Ma to climb a tree
sit cross-legged in the middle of the street
or cartwheel up the sidewalk
ignoring folks strolling up and down the block.
That's just the kind of mom James Henry and me got.
At least the one we had most our lives.

Sitting on a corner bench
I asked why she wasn't doing any of those things.

Ma moved closer to me.
"No one stays the same."
She smiled.
"I went into the ocean
    and came out different."

But different can be good, she said
twisting the ends of her long black hair.
"That's what I learned from my accident."

Ma went into the ocean last year to save Dog
and nearly drowned.
Brother blamed himself since
it was his idea to go to the beach
late
in the dark
under a blue moon.

I grew up overnight.

Had to. I was needed.

Ma sat close
combing my hair with her fingers.
    "I'm okay. Fine. My old self again.
Close to it anyway.
Walking two miles a day
talking more than I should
teaching young folks to express themselves
    in trouble at another school."
She laughed.

Ma taught down South.
Nearly got fired until she got hurt.
She's better
but different.
Everybody says so, she told me.

WHAT MA COULD SEE THAT I COULDN'T

"You got sick. Everything changed.
    Now it's changing again,"
I told Ma.

"How?" Ma said.

I couldn't say exactly
    so I brought up Brother.
"I miss him . . .
he always wanted to be close by me
now he takes forever to answer my letters."

Ma said it's because he's growing up.
Making his own choices.
    Ones that suit him better.
"You free to do the same.
But I don't think this is about James Henry.
Is it?
Nor that girl Lisa
when it comes down to it."

I jump to my feet. "Cousin told you about her?"

"She didn't have to.
I have eyes."

UNDERNEATH THE TREE WITH FAMILY

Ma made her way over to a tree.
Not to climb like she would have before
but to sit under.
I could see her thinking
pondering
looking sad
smiling finally.

"Come here, baby girl."

I joined her under a weeping willow
with branches down to the ground.

"Time changes everything . . ."

Her hand found mine.

". . . turns green leaves brown
sends the earth around the moon
watches the moon go from a quarter to full
to blue
to red or gold
whipping up tides and storms.
Takes a six-pound baby girl
    turns her beautiful and tall as her ma
puts meat on her bones
watches her go from one grade to the other.
One state to another.
Grows her up inside and out."

"Are you talking about me, Ma?"

"Of course."

I think about it all.
The times I was in the forest
walking in the ocean
swimming
fighting bees
milking cows at Gran's.
Now I'm here, free to be myself, only it isn't easy, I admit.
"I try to make you proud, Ma.
To be
    a good student
help others
without being asked
to write regularly
to Gran
you
Daddy and Brother."

"It must get tiring."

"It does . . . sometimes." My insides ached.

Ma hugged me forever, it seemed.
    I come out and say it.
"I don't fit.
They're different from me.
Cousin has her favorites.
I'll never catch up."
    More tears follow the rest.
"Oh, Ma
maybe I should go home."

Her arms soothed me some. "Hattie Mae, you don't have to be

perfect
or like anyone else but yourself."
In fact, she said,
I had her permission
to trip and skin my knees from time to time
to forget that she ever had that accident
to only think good thoughts about Dog
to not hold on so tight to things I couldn't change anyhow
to just be me, Hattie Mae.
As studious or raggedy as I wanted
with tears in my pants or a tiara on my head
with holes in my shoes or dressed in a ball gown
my hair a mess or with curls aplenty
forgetting sometimes to do what was right by other people
but never myself.

My eyes closed
I tried
to see myself before Ma went into the ocean
before we even met Dog
or I came to school here.
    I was *me* then.
Hattie Mae
more like Ma, now that I thought about it.
Free as the wind.

Then I changed.
Stood ramrod straight.
Took charge.
Don't remember nobody asking me to.

"Why'd I change, Ma?"

Maybe I should be asking a different question,

she said,
like how come I'm opposed
to being my own true self
regardless of what the world thinks?

BIRDS OF A FEATHER

My arms turned into a string of pearls
around her neck.
People walked by, stared and smiled.
We make a beautiful pair, Ma said
hurrying up the street
    with me following.

Block after block
it was Ma and me.
flying side by side
laughing
free
to travel in whichever direction we pleased
she reminded me.

COMING AND GOING

We were almost home
when we ran into Adelaide and her mother.
I introduced them
blushed when Mrs. Carolyn started bragging about me.

"Your Hattie helped my Adelaide see
that new places are just new opportunities
to make new friends." Mrs. Carolyn pinched my chin.
"She is generous and kind
a hard worker besides and a credit to those who raised her."
    She gave me a giant-sized hug.
"Leaving the South
coming North, all the changes
    different values and ways of living. It's a lot."
She wiped her eyes. "We appreciate you, Hattie.
And I wanted your ma to know it."

The next day
packing to leave, Ma stayed quiet.
Me too.
Then she disappeared
said she had a meeting downstairs with Cousin.
    Ma was gone when Cousin Abigail apologized.
She promised to do better by me.
Neither one of them ever said what the talk was about exactly.

WHAT BERT OVERHEARD AT THE TABLE

At night in bed
Bert finally brought up something Cousin Abigail said
while Ma was here.

"She's your cousin, isn't she?
That's what Lisa has against you."

I took a chance. "Lisa doesn't know.
If she did
Cousin and me would be kicked out of here in two shakes.
Lisa's father would make sure of it."

"It's like being in a movie.
    A mystery movie where the secrets keep coming."
Her protest came to mind, but I was too tired to bring it up.

EAVESDROPPING AGAIN

They were back
members of Cousin's club
only this time
there was a man with them.
One by one Cousin introduced
him to everyone else.
He was the president of Douglass Hospital
    Dr. John P. Kennedy.
    They are having their troubles but trying to stay afloat as
    well. "One can
learn as much from a house on fire as they can from a newly
built home."
    Six times a year the women bring a special guest, I learned.
The next person will be the head of Mercy Hospital
followed by one of our neighbors, Marion Stubbs Thomas, the president
of a new organization, Jack and Jill. Cousin said in due time we
girls will be members as well.

Soon enough
I was asleep, though.
Not that they were boring.
Bert interrupting my sleep last night was at the root of it all.

TAKING THE LEAD

Alabaster had to make a few deliveries.
We both hopped on the bike.
Me with my coat buttoned tight.
Him asking me to pedal a little slower.

The street and sidewalks were slushy
from last night's snow
and a skyful of sunshine this morning.

I told Alabaster to hold on tighter
if he didn't want to end up on the ground
like I did that time.

"Should we walk, maybe
    and push the bike?" he asked.

I laughed.
Swerved and wobbled with the bike
a time or two.

"I'm mighty glad you decided to stay
Miss Hattie, even if your driving leaves a lot to be desired."
    "Me too, Alabaster.
Me too."

DAYDREAMING

I could come in, he told me
or stay outdoors in the cold
and wait on him to return.

I handed over the bag of shoes.
    "I'll wait."
Stamping my cold feet
I blew smoke.

Alabaster lifted a knocker
announcing himself.
    A man let him into the house.

I shivered.
Rubbed my hands together to warm 'em.

Wiping my drippy nose
I imagined this was my house
my servant escorting Alabaster inside.
I could see myself
rich
throwing elegant parties
every night of the week.
    Ma would say it's okay to dream
to hunger for things
long as you don't break the law
or hurt people.

WHAT ALABASTER DOES WITH HIS MONEY

Alabaster came back flipping a quarter in his hand.

"A tip," he said
pocketing it, then hopping on his bike.
    "I'll add it to the rest."

Later I learned he puts his tips in a pot
underneath the kitchen sink
right along with his mother's loose change.
They plan to use the money to send his cousin to
Y camp, overnight for seven days. A first for kids like us.
It costs five bucks a week.
    He and his ma have nearly every cent of it, he said.
His cousin will need lots of extras too
sheets
a lantern, a flashlight, soap
a change of clothes every other day of the week
'cause boat trips, camping out
trekking through the woods at night
can sure put a hurting on you and your things, he told me.
    When he stopped at the next light
he turned a nickel over to me. Smiling. "The driver
deserves a tip too."
    That's when I told him about Hattie's Helpers.

A WELCOME DONATION

Because of the cold
I don't see Adelaide and her mother much.
Today
I went to their house in the Seventh Ward.
Her father answered
wearing painter's pants
stained
holding a wet brush in his hand.
    "Can I help ya?"

"I'm looking for Adelaide."
    I held up my books.
"She's coming to our school next year.
    I'm here to help her prepare."

"Well, now. You must be Hattie Mae.
    Those two talk about you night and day."
He said to be careful. All the walls were wet.
"You might want to go next door to Miss Rita's house
    to study," he told Adelaide and me.

Wouldn't you know it, Miss Rita knew my name.
Made space for us at the kitchen table.
    She sat a spell while I taught Adelaide a little Latin.
"You think I could learn to speak another language?"
Miss Rita asked me.
    I told her I didn't see why not.
"People can learn at any age. Even if they're old."

She laughed.

Me and Adelaide went to work.

Afterward, I told her I enjoyed helping people.
She jumped out the chair. "I'm a helper too." And left the house then returned with two pennies. "Now you can help more girls, right?"

COMING CLEAN

The next day I went to Cousin's office
with a big, giant question.
   "Why did you bring me here?"

She asked Mrs. Britain to excuse us.

"I don't care that they don't like me.
But it isn't fair
to bring someone to your school
when no one else there looks like them
and girls protest against them."

"But we're all Negroes."

"That's not enough," I told her.

TALKING TO COUSIN
UNTIL I RUN OUT OF WORDS

In the city
our people are fighting
    for their fair share
of jobs and everything else,
I told Cousin.
And winning lots of times.
Sitting
with my fists in my lap
I told her I'd been fighting since I got here
with girls like Lisa
who don't think I belong.

"But I do."

I interrupted Cousin Abigail
when she tried to speak.

"I want other girls to attend our school
like me
other boys too."

I thought about Adelaide.
If she is hardworking and studious
then she has as much right to be here
as Lisa
me
and the rest.

We all deserve the chance at a first-rate
education.
And I deserve to be around girls

who come from my neck of the woods
those familiar with what I know
harvest season
canning
spring planting
banjo playing
square dancing
roads that don't end
sitting high atop a tree when it rains in the spring.

Explaining yourself and your ways
is a hard chore with no end in sight, I told her.
"I remember what Ma told me once.
    Everyone is needed.
Everyone is deserving.
We just have to give one another a chance."

Cousin said she agreed.

THE TRUTH AND NOTHING BUT THE TRUTH

At the table, discussing the news
Cousin Abigail brought up
the volunteer list.
I mentioned Hattie's Helpers.
    What it is. The good it can do.
How a scholarship is already set up.
"Small . . . but still . . ."
I told them about tutoring Adelaide.
Mending clothes and passing 'em on.
    "I have a list of other things
helpers can do . . . if . . . people want to join . . ."
    Bert's hand went up.
Two other girls asked how they could be helpers too.
Two girls asked to be dismissed.
Lisa laughed.
Said it wasn't a real charity
and I should not be allowed to
list it as a volunteer organization.

"And why not?"
Cousin fixed her eyes on Lisa.
    "Miss Abigail's girls think outside the box.
Cousin, I'm proud of you."

Lisa stood up.
    "What did you say?"

"Lisa. I do not think I like your tone."
    They all heard it, she said.

Cousin Abigail looked around the table.
"Heard what?"

"You called her 'Cousin.' You two are related."
	Lisa was disgusted, you could tell.

Cousin Abigail looked at me.
I nodded. "Yes, we are."

WHAT DOESN'T COME OUT IN THE WASH

Over dessert
no one spoke a word
except Miss Abigail.

"Hattie Mae is my cousin
on my father's side.
I hope no one here
thought I was playing favorites."

Her eyes found Lisa.

"I certainly tried my best not to.
Though it did not serve Hattie Mae
very well.
I am told that a few of you think
she received more than her fair share
of my attention
and perhaps high marks she did not earn.

"Well
I am here to assure you it never happened.
She is a very hard worker
deserves what grades she earned.
I apologize to you—one and all—
your parents and Hattie Mae also.

"A letter will go home to them soon."

Cousin pushed her chair back.
Walked up to me.
Knelt down.
And asked me to accept her apologies.

"By not
claiming you as family
I denied your worth and dignity.
And unknowingly pitted you against the other girls
    Though never intentionally.
I hope you do not leave."
She lifted her hand
like she was going to give a pledge.
    "I apologize to all of you and
promise to do better."

MAKING THE NEWS ONE MORE TIME

"Did you hear . . . ?"
Bert barged into the library like she was being chased.
Out of breath
she threw her books on the desk I was sitting at.
"Two . . . girls . . .
packed up and left . . . just this minute."
She ran over to the window pointing.
"Eiffel Tower and Dorothy." She faced my way.
"Come see."

I met her at the window.
There they were, getting into two different cars
Cadillacs.
For the first time I noticed
a newspaper under Bert's arm.
She unfolded it at my table.

"It says here Marigold and Ella
will be attending
the Philadelphia High School for Girls.
    One of the best."

But they are still enrolled, I pointed out.
Or are more girls leaving?
    Emptying out the school a few at a time.

"Hold on, there's more," Bert said.
"Another article about us, over here."

BREAKING NEWS ABOUT OUR SCHOOL

To our readers who have been filling
our mailboxes with questions and concerns
please know that we hear and listen to you.

Miss Abigail's School for Exceptional Young Ladies
is at the heart of the matter.
More parents have withdrawn their daughters.
There is talk from reliable sources
of favoritism by the headmistress, deception and lying
using finances unwisely, perhaps even illegally,
standards and quality dropping
parents pulling out their children because of fights and the like.
Should girls of lower means even be admitted?
    I pose the question because we need to.
Rumors or the truth, we must get to the bottom of this
for our children's sake and our community's reputation.

We strongly urge Miss Abigail to answer these questions
    or prepare to lose more students.

PROTESTING LISA

Since Lisa heard the news about me
she's hardly been to class
or taken meals with us.
I don't know if she's disappointed
that I'm related to Cousin
or if she's sad because her best friends are gone
    and she has to put up with the rest of us.

She was in the parlor
    all by her lonesome
when Bert told me to "go in there."

"No."

"Now who is protesting whom?"

THE TRUTH ABOUT THINGS

I went upstairs.
Put on my best dress
returned
and sat down near Lisa.

She did not say a word
    at first anyhow.
        "You are not wanted.
Go away," she finally said.

I almost did.
But I've got Gran's blood in me
Ma's tough ways.
"You've been trying to boss me
long enough."

Her father was on his way
to withdraw her from school, I learned.
Miss Abigail's School for Exceptional Young Ladies is no longer
good enough for her, Lisa said.
She was headed to France to attend boarding school.
"My father selected it.
    He will be here any day now."

"No he won't and you know it."

A QUESTION I COULD NOT ANSWER

She didn't make a sound.
    I moved closer.
"Are you ashamed because of your parents' divorce?
    You shouldn't be."
    I moved closer still.
"It wasn't your fault, the circumstances
your parents found themselves in.
You're loved nonetheless, I just know it
regardless of if they're together or not.
And once your father collects himself
    you'll see him all the time.
He seems like that kind of father.
    He's likely sad . . . down to the bone. Just like you."

A sound came out of her
like wind passing through trees
    like a sneeze she didn't want to let go.
Then it came
a whisper.
Words she had to repeat twice
before I could hear her.
    "Why? Why doesn't anybody love me?"

EVERYTHING YOU WANT TO KNOW ABOUT LISA

In her room
standing on a stool
Lisa took a blue velvet hatbox
from the top shelf of her closet.
Sitting next to me on her bed, she took the top off.
Showed me
pictures of her in Paris under the Eiffel Tower
with her parents.
I reached into the box
pulled out a picture of them in Chicago at the World's Fair
    another one with them in London at the River Thames.
They were paddling up the Schuylkill River
    in a canoe in the picture in her hand.

"That's us
holding hands near the
Arch in Saint Louis."
    Her eyes watered.

In every picture
she looked rich
wanted.
Satisfied with herself.
The picture of them at the Macy's parade
in New York City at Christmastime may be my favorite.

She went to the closet again.
Took out a box the same size as the other one.
It was covered in yellow crepe with pleats on the side
and a big satin bow held the top and bottom together.
It was filled with baby things.
    Out came

a dress Lisa's gran knitted for her to wear
    the minute she was born.
Lisa shook a rattle
picked up a lock of hair
and the ribbon her gran tied around it.

She was careful picking up
a gold bracelet about the size of a baby's fist.
    "I wore this until I couldn't."

Her gran saved everything, she told me.
    "I miss her and my grandfather too. They passed on.
You are the luckiest, Hattie Mae. You still have family."

I asked about her grandparents on her mother's side.

"They live somewhere in California.
Father loss contact after my mother died."

I took her by the hand.
    "Well, let's find their address
and write to them."

She looked surprised.
    "Do you think they would want
to hear from me? I never did."
    "You won't know unless you try."
Right then and there we went to Cousin Abigail's office
and got the information we needed.

GRAN'S RING BACK WHERE IT BELONGS

Lisa went over to her dresser
and opened the music box.
    I was surprised when she took out the ring
and set it in my hand.

"I apologize, Hattie.
    It belongs to you and your family.
I think . . . I was jealous of that."

I ran to my room, thankful.
    Inside my closet
I grabbed the twine.
Lisa, right behind me, tied it around my neck
once I hung the ring on it.

We both forgot ourselves, I think
and hugged a good, long time.

WHAT HAPPENED OUTSIDE OUR FRONT DOOR

"What's that noise?" Lisa said
running over to the window.
We couldn't see a thing
    but the noise got louder
like people arguing
    so we ran downstairs.

Outside our building
a woman was walking back and forth carrying a sign
protesting us
telling the world our school should be shut down.

SAVING OUR SCHOOL

Cousin Abigail, Mrs. Britain and Mrs. Santiago all spoke to the woman.
But it did no good.
She told them she was determined
to return with friends
tomorrow
along with a bigger sign.
She wanted us shut down
because of the newspaper article.
    We were not fit for the neighborhood, she said.
And to prove it
five more people showed up.
They were parents of students at our school. Neighbors too.
They met with the teachers for hours.

At the end of the day
I went from one bedroom door to the next
knocking.

"Meet me in my room.
    It's an emergency."

Lisa was the last to arrive.
She would not sit down.
Standing by the door, she looked out of place.

This is our school
ours.
"It is up to us to save it," I said.

CEO OF EVERYTHING

Everyone had an idea except Lisa.
I took notes
like the women in Cousin Abigail's social club.
Imagined a sign over my head
HATTIE MAE, CEO OF EVERYTHING.

Bert's idea was to have all of us write to the *Tribune*
let them know how unfair they were being to us.

Angelina thought we shouldn't do anything.
Just hope for the best and see what became
of the school next year.

Lisa didn't want any part of it.

STANDING UP FOR OUR SCHOOL

The next Sunday
I called another meeting
after a phone call from Ma
who said Cousin's troubles had made it to Detroit
and down South.

"Christmas is around the corner.
Should we send for you early?"

"I couldn't, Ma.
Not now. Cousin needs me.
Our school has a black eye
    and for no good reason."

I was on my way upstairs
when I overheard Cousin's conversation.
She was nearly in tears.
    "What will I do?
Our reputation is in tatters.
When that happens
sometimes money dries up
student numbers dwindle.
What if we have to close our doors?
This building . . . my father has owned it forever."

ANSWERS TO OUR PROBLEM

Reading the *Tribune* the next day
I saw his name.
Dr. Kennedy, the man from Cousin's meeting
and president of staff at Douglass Hospital.
    I just knew he'd want to help Cousin Abigail.
Besides
he is a man used to solving big problems, a surgeon.
And even though there'd been talk of merging the hospital
with Mercy
Douglass was still planning to hold a fundraiser, Cousin told us,
to open their doors to the public to show the good they do
at the hospital and their dental clinic.

MY MEETING WITH THE PRESIDENT

Alabaster was delivering shoes
up the street when I walked up to him.
"May I use your bike? Please.
It's an emergency.
　　I need to get to Douglass Hospital."
With the *Tribune* under my arm I explained things.
It was Alabaster's idea to go to Mercy Hospital too.
What harm could it do, he said.
　　I took off on his bike.
Pages of the paper got away from me,
flying like they had wings.
I stopped and pulled myself together.
By the time I arrived at the hospital, I looked perfectly put
together.

Patent leather shoes make the best sound on hospital floors.
Tap. Tap. Tap.
Sounded like I had taps on my shoes.
Doctors and nurses smiled at me.
Patients moved out my way.
When I got to his office
　　his secretary said,
"And who are you, little miss?"
　　Then she asked where my parents were.

I explained how important it was
for me to meet with the president right now, today.
At first she said it was absolutely impossible.
　　She asked if I knew he was a very important
busy man with back-to-back meetings, surgery the next
morning.

"I am one of Miss Abigail's girls."
  "Oh, are you?"

I set the paper on her desk
opened to the page with the article on it.
"I have to see him. It's important."

I know he has a lot on his mind, I said.
I read about Douglass Hospital all the time in the *Tribune*.
  "Couldn't you just tell him I'm here?"

MEN FROM THE PYRAMID CLUB

I explained everything to him.

He's a busy man
but said he could squeeze in a few meetings
if Cousin Abigail was agreeable.

"I'm sure she is, sir."

Fingering his chin, he said
he would even speak with members
    of the Pyramid Club.
"Who?"

"A group of professionals
doctors, lawyers, business owners
with thriving practices right here in our community.
They may even donate money to the school."

I asked for their names.

"No need," he said. "I will speak to them on your behalf."
I shook his hand and took off.
Before I knew it
I was at Mercy, meeting with Dr. Eugene Hinson.
Oh, what a day.

MAKING US GIRLS FEEL LEFT OUT

First the board showed up
then the women from Cousin's club
    every single one of them, Cousin bragged
and a few more women besides.
Next came the presidents of both hospitals
along with men in tweed coats and dark suits
looking stately and important.
Together
they filled both dining room tables
threw around ideas
using a chalkboard
    lined paper
and someone to take dictation.
We girls were permitted to sit in the adjoining room
if we did not speak or make unnecessary noises.
That didn't seem fair.

I raised my hand.

"What about us? Don't we get a say?"
    Bert stood up beside me.
"This is our school. But you are leaving us out."
    Side by side, ten of us held arms.
Lisa was the last one.
        "She is trying," I heard Bert say.

Cousin told us to be prepared to share our ideas
next Monday.

HATTIE'S HELPERS:
PEOPLE WHO CARE ABOUT PEOPLE

We left the meeting
    marched upstairs
with me at the head of the line.
Turning left
we ended up in our room—me and Bert's.
Girls sat on the beds
on the floor
by the door
crowded around each other.
    Lisa was at the window, staring out.
A few complained.
"Stop it," I said.
    "All we need is a plan."

I squeezed past Bert
    went into my closet
opened the suitcase
came back with Gran's sewing tin
and Hattie's Helpers patches.
    Lisa read out loud,
"'Hattie's Helpers.'"
    Her nose wrinkled.

"This patch means we are helpers
leaders," I said.
"Girls doing good for other girls and our community.
    If you want to be a helper and save our school
raise your hand."
Lots of hands went up.
Bert and I pinned patches on the others
    but only those who wanted to wear them.

"The grown-ups
aren't the only ones with good ideas,"
I told them.

Lisa always sounds sour.
"It takes money, you know."

I emptied my Mason jar on the bed. "We can start with this."

A SOLUTION TO OUR PROBLEM

Sitting at her desk, Bert recited a poem for English class
the way she'd done all week.
She knew it by heart
    me too now.

I threw a pillow at her head to make her shut up.
She kept right at it.
I thought about yesterday's meeting
    our school's situation
and Monday coming
none of us with any ideas.

"Please, Bert, be quiet!"

This time she threw a pillow at me.
    "I do not want to be in the front of the class babbling.
I practice so that people will
want to hear me and think I'm amazing.
They might even want to pay to see me one day."

That's when it hit me
we could put on a show and invite the whole neighborhood
for a small fee.
Recite poetry by
Countee Cullen
    Anne Spencer
Maybe even Shakespeare.
We study them in class
    it would be easy, I thought.
The money would go to the school
    to start scholarships for students.

I opened my mouth to tell Bert
only she started talking first.
   "I *protest* because I want everybody
to be able to go to the movies, sit wherever they want
   and get whatever job they please.
   Besides, it's only right. Something my mother's
side of the family does all the time in one way or the other.
Plus, when I'm acting, I want everybody to come and see me."

I ran over and hugged her.

RUNNING OUT OF TIME

For the next three days
they talked about enrollment
allowing boys to attend
fundraising to purchase a new building
hiring additional staff
getting positive articles written about us in the *Tribune*.

After a break they thought up more ideas
    said Cousin's school needed the NAACP's support behind
    it
that the board should reach out to the YWCA and Eleanor
Roosevelt
    because of their commitment to girls like us and
take a meeting with the mayor and city council
because it never hurts to have politicians in your corner
    spreading the word about the good your organization does
joining forces with you economically.

It would take a long while to turn the ship around
I heard one of them say.

But we didn't have time.
And right then that woman returned
    with two other people
protesting us
and they all had signs.

HATTIE'S HELPERS UP TO THE TASK

We walked into Cousin's meeting
each wearing the same colors
    cream-colored dresses
and red sweaters
with Hattie's Helpers patches sewn on 'em.

Carrying notebooks and pencils
looking serious as the Women of the Future Club members
we lined the wall.
It was Lisa's idea to practice
    practice
    practice
after school, all week long.
    Finally she asked for a patch.

I introduced everyone
beginning with myself.
In my mind I saw my name
Hattie Mae, Chairman of the Board.
"This is our school
and we want to do our part," I told them.

"Miss Abigail
we know the school has plans
but we do also," Bert said.
    We all shared our ideas with the group.
"We want permission to do somethings on our own,"
I told them.
    "But, girls—"

Lisa spoke up. "You always say you are
developing leaders—"

Bert interrupted. "Then let us lead."

She went quiet for a while. "It seems you have it all worked out."
Cousin looked proud.

Miss New York nodded
encouraged us
when we got stuck or felt nervous.

Dr. Kennedy was the first to clap.
Everyone else followed
stood up
said we had a marvelous idea
one that could be implemented right away.

LISA HAS A CHANGE OF HEART

It was three of us girls
plus Cousin and a Christmas tree
in the parlor, near the fireplace
    dressed in our robes and pajamas.
    Lisa was in the corner
on the other side of the room.

Cousin handed us each a present
    notebooks with our names
engraved on them.
    No one seemed angry
when I got mine.
HATTIE'S HELPERS
A VOLUNTEER ORGANIZATION

I hugged her tight.

Everyone got a picture from me.
I spent all weekend drawing 'em.
    Bert in our room at her desk
smiling.
Cousin in class teaching.
I drew Lisa sitting with her good friends
    Eiffel Tower and Dorothy in front of our school.

How'd I know it would make her cry.
Up she jumped, running out the room.
Taking the steps to the second floor.
Handing out jewelry boxes when she returned.
I got a string of pink pearls.
Bert got a fancy bracelet with puppy dogs surrounding it.
    "And that girl . . . the one who stares at our school a lot.

Maybe she would like this." It was a white hat with fur balls on each tie.
And white mittens to match.
"I have so many things I have never worn . . ."

Lisa ran out of words, I think. But not Bert.
"Well, now you are one of Hattie's Helpers too."

MAKING PEOPLE PROUD

Hattie's Helpers
A Volunteer Organization

Bert made the sign
and hung it on our bedroom door.
There were nine names
including mine and my title, President and CEO.
    I stared at it off and on all day long.
Thought about Seed County
and my family.
How proud they would be of me.

JANUARY 1939

For once the *Tribune*
had something good to say about us.
And it came on the first day of the New Year.

There are many changes afoot at
Miss Abigail's School for Exceptional Young Ladies,
but people seem to be keeping most of them
under wraps.

But there is a buzz around a student-led initiative
called Hattie's Helpers.
The organization is holding a recital
inviting area youth ages 12–16 to participate.
All donations will benefit new students to the school.
Posters go up today.
    Contributions of all kinds will be accepted.

Our community must lift all boats
not just a few, so
donate.
Donate.
Donate.

WELCOME, ONE AND ALL

With our hands covering our mouths
and scarfs over our heads
we braved the cold
    and got the job done.
Up went the posters
    on poles
      in store windows
          where clothes and food were sold
      on church bulletins in big churches
like Tindley Temple on South Broad Street and
    inside schools.

By the time we got home
four girls were at our front door
along with two boys.

I took their names
since Cousin wasn't there.

"Does this mean we will be admitted into your school?"
Nelson wanted to know.

"Anybody with talent and smarts will be allowed
to participate in the recital," I said.
    "Miss Abigail takes care of school matters."

GOOD NEIGHBORS

Alabaster showed up the next day
with two nickels and a quarter.
Later a stranger knocked on the door.
    Opening it
I recognized him right away.
It was the man from outside the museum.
"You girls is a credit to the community.
Here's two pennies.
Useful for something, I hope."

I couldn't help myself
I hugged him.
The next day our neighbor Mrs. Conner came into the house
with three men behind her.
One carrying a basket of potatoes
    shipped from Maine, he told us.
The next man had a ham slung over his shoulders.
The third was hauling a case of canned corn.
    They wanted to make sure we could provide a good
meal to those attending our recital. "Hang on to the rest for
whenever you
need it."
    "Lordy," Cousin said, showing 'em the way to the pantry.

Alabaster's mother insisted on contributing too.
    She would make a pan of fried tomatoes and okra.
Charge ten cents a plate.
I did not find myself looking forward to it.

CHOOSING OUR OWN PARTS

We were packed in the parlor
like cookies in a tin.
Sitting on the sofa
in wing-back chairs
and on the floor
    which is never agreeable to Cousin.

Lisa handed out sheets of paper
to me first
Alabaster last.
I unfolded mine.
"It's a poem. By Claude McKay," I said.

Bert opened hers next.
It was a long one. A speech
by Eleanor Roosevelt for the twenty-fifth
anniversary of the Girl Scouts.
    Bert found it herself.

"You think you can remember all that? I couldn't," I said.
    She held it up for everyone to see.
"An actress has to memorize long scenes."

If she nailed it, then maybe her father wouldn't mind
her attending the University of Pennsylvania for theater
one day, she told us.

Alabaster leaned over my shoulder, reading the poem.
    "'To One Coming North.'" He pulled at his necktie.
"I thought the recital was supposed to be fun, Miss Hattie.
We will put everybody to sleep.

And what would that do to help the school's reputation?" he wanted to know.

BERT AND I GO CHECK ON LISA

"Listen. Can't you hear her?"
Bert pressed her ear to the door.
"It's Lisa. Crying. I know it."
    I got out of bed and joined her.
Soon we opened the door
stopped in the hall
    in the dark
and listened.
It was her all right.

I tapped on the door. "Lisa. Lisa.
If you don't let us in
I'll go get Cousin."

A minute later
there she was
her face dripping tears.

HOW IT FEELS TO MISS YOUR FAMILY

Leave the light off, she told us.

I sat down on one side of her bed.
Bert sat on the other.

We promised not to tell if she told us
what was bothering her, I said.

"I miss my father.
    My family
everybody. But nobody misses me."

TAKING MATTERS INTO MY OWN HANDS

Dear Dr. Connolly,
  If you could
you should come and visit Lisa.
She needs you.
A busy father is like having none at all.

I stuffed the letter in an envelope.
Took it to the door
left it for the postman to pick up.
And crossed my fingers.

OUR FINAL REHEARSAL

Alabaster threw a green marble in the air
and tried to catch it with his mouth.

Bert's eyes dug into him
then she clapped for our attention.
    "Are we ready?"
It was a question she asked all week
not expecting us to answer
but it quieted us down.

We were in the school library
preparing to recite our poems
perfectly this time.

Bert started with the students
whose poems had the fewest words.
Lisa said a parrot could recite those.

Sharon went first.
Headed to the front of the room
shaking in her boots.
She never skipped a word or stuttered.
Everybody clapped for her once she was done.

"She mumbles.
Did you hear it?" Bert said.

I didn't notice.
I was too busy
being nervous for my own self.

Alabaster surprised us

projecting perfectly, Bert told him.
"Enunciating flawlessly."

He could have busted his buttons
he looked so proud of himself.
Lisa went next
    head up, back straight.
"I did an outstanding
    impressive job. The best," she said later.

I went last.
Alabaster repeated himself.
    "Aren't we going to do anything fun?
When y'all talk that Shakespeare talk
I don't know what you're saying. And Mom won't either."

ONE LAST CUSTOMER
AT THE DOOR

All day Saturday and Sunday
they came
    one
by
    one
whole families at a time.

"We read it in the newspaper
    that everyone is invited."

"Pay what you can,"
    Cousin would tell them.

Alabaster and another boy
were lions at the door
holding baskets and smiling
    while the money went in.
Some paid a dime
some ten dollars
others paid fifty cents.
In exchange Bert gave them
a piece of paper with the word Paid
    stamped in the corner.

It was also their invitation to get in
next weekend.

They stood and stood
waited
    quiet as mice
    even with the snow

blowing in circles
raining down on them the whole time.

Mr. Gage shoveled around their feet.
Mrs. Dreamer offered them hot peanuts
told them to hold on to the shells.

"Our pastor said we ought to offer our support," one woman said.
"My daughter's teacher told us about this," someone else told us.
    "We see your girls.
Fine and respectable.
    Good examples for our daughters."

Cousin looked proud as a peacock.

Adelaide gave us three pennies and skipped off.
She was the last one, so I closed the door.
Then I heard a knock
    and opened it wide.

"My husband and I received your letter." It was Lisa's
grandparents.
"We were not sure Lisa would want to receive us. It has been
such a long time.
    But then we saw this." She held up the newspaper.
"We just had to come and see our Lisa.
Please accept our money. I will take ten tickets, please."

LISA GETS HER WISH

"Lisa," I hollered. "Lisa, you're wanted."

She came down the steps the way she always did
floating.
Stopping when she saw her grandparents.
Before we knew it
she was running to them
    crying
    hugging
kissing them.
    They all talked at the same time.

"I love you.
    I miss you."

"It was my fault," her grandmother said.

    "Why doesn't anybody love me?"

"We do.
    Let that be enough for now," her grandfather told her.

THE BEST PRESENT EVER

The next day
outside our bedroom door
I found a silver music box
with a note inside:
    Hattie Mae Jenkins, Mistress of Ceremonies.

BRAGGING ABOUT US

What Ma said while she was here is true.
    Change ain't bad.
Just different.

The news of the day
was about our school this time
and how the *Tribune* wrote something
positive about us twice in one month.

If Philadelphia is to be the mecca
we envision
we must make room for one and all
ensure our youth receive first-rate educations
and experiences that too often only the elite
have access to. Therefore
congratulations to
Miss Abigail's School for Exceptional Young Ladies
for its bold decision to admit
fourteen new students
seven girls
seven boys
at the start of the school year.

Each child shall attend tuition-free
due to the generosity of fifteen donors
along with churches, social clubs and
private organizations, politicians and even the city.
And let's not leave out Hattie's Helpers
    whose event kicks off tomorrow.
Good luck, everyone!

OUR BIG DAY

Alabaster shined everyone's shoes.
When?
We do not know.
We woke up and they were done
    lined up in one long row at the bottom of the stairs.

Cousin and Mrs. Britain
brushed and combed our hair
not trusting one of us to get it
    straight and shiny.

"Pair up." Cousin clapped
waited until we were lined up by height.

The two of them marched up and down each row
tucking shirts into trousers
retying shoelaces
insisting that we stand up tall and erect.

We were putting on our coats
when I remembered
that I was forgetting something.

WHAT I SAW IN THE MIRROR

Cousin told me I was being
most unladylike, running up the steps
two at a time.

In the hallway upstairs
I tripped and fell down.
Soon enough I had what I'd come for.
Gran's necklace.
I took the ring off the twine
undid the clasp on the string of pearls I was wearing.
And slid Gran's ring onto the necklace
    before I put it back on.

I looked myself over in the mirror.
Twirled
watched my gown puff out.
A Christmas present from Ma and Daddy.

Periwinkle blue
with sequins that sparkled like stars
it stopped at my ankles
    tickled my shoes
the ones Alabaster gave me.

"I did not shame the family, Gran," I said
holding on to the ring.
"Not much, anyways.
    And I grew some, no, a whole bunch."
I gave myself a hug.
    "I like being Miss Hattie Mae."

BACK TO MOTHER'S HOUSE

Walking for blocks
heads up
proud
we heard the claps
saw cars stop
listened to them honk for us.

"Never forget," Cousin told us
from the head of the line.
"You are the best this nation has to offer.
Much is expected of you."

Outside of Mother Bethel Church
I got a chill
but not from the weather.
I was thinking about the first day I'd met her.
What Mr. Gage said about the church being his North Star
    and how much I would like Philadelphia.
He was right about everything.

A COMMUNITY GATHERING

The sign outside said:
PROCEEDS TO BENEFIT HATTIE'S HELPERS.
    We'd made two hundred dollars so far. A fortune.
After people paid for food, Cousin said we might clear
another hundred.
The money will help new students with clothes
and to travel back home for out-of-towners.

"Ready?"
Mr. Gage met me at the front door.

It was standing room only.
Like the whole city showed up.
I waved at the presidents of Douglass and Mercy Hospitals
and anybody else I could recognize.
I heard Bert whisper,
    "My father came. He's over there."

I stopped and spoke to him.
Alabaster gave me a kiss on the cheek
on his way to his seat.

I started running after I saw Daddy.
"Gran. Ma. Brother." I hugged them one by one.
"Why didn't you say you were coming?"

Brother, dressed in a black suit
    pulled at his shirt collar.
"We're here to surprise you."
    I held on to him like I'd never let go.
Gran said, "Knock 'em dead, baby."
Daddy winked. Told me I looked beautiful.

Uncle and his wife smiled.
Ma said she knew I could do anything I put my mind to.

On my way to the front of the church
Lisa stopped me.
"Do you want to meet my family? There are two rows of them including my father." She hugged me tight.

    Her father took my hand.
"Sometimes adults need a little prodding, thanks."

NOT SO FAST, HATTIE MAE

I never get nervous.
But there I was at the podium shaking so hard I had to hold my hands tight
    and bite my bottom lip to keep it from trembling.

People started whispering. Ma stood up, as if ready to be with me.

Lisa yelled across the church. "You can do it, Hattie Mae." Bert joined her.
Before I knew it, every single one of Miss Abigail' s girls were on their feet, including
Adelaide.
Clapping and cheering me on.
Lifting me up in my time of need.
I hear myself begin:

"Good afternoon, everyone. My name is Hattie Mae. I am your Mistress of Ceremonies and the President of Hattie's Helpers.
I hope you enjoy our presentation today."

I explained how this happened because we
all came together.
I talked about the girls at school.
Donations from neighbors and strangers.
I mentioned Alabaster. "Because of him
there'll be all kinds of entertainment tonight
from poetry to double Dutch."

I looked out at the crowd
    family and friends and folks from all over.

I thought about all the people
who'd come to this city long before me.
Helpers
when you think about it.
    Supporting each other and making their mark on the city.

And now I am too.
Hattie Mae Jenkins
    A Girl on Her Way Up.

AUTHOR'S NOTE

I am a daughter of Philadelphia, born to a daughter of Philadelphia. My family's roots on my mother's side go back to the twenties as far as we know, when my grandma Marie arrived from Saint Michael's, Maryland. Philly is in my blood, you could say. It is where I was born and attended school. I grew up on a narrow street filled with homes of families who went on to live on that block for generations. Block parties, a staple of the city, were a summertime treat, where families set tables on sidewalks and closed off streets from traffic. They would cool off under the fireplug; grill food and eat together; play cards and reminisce late into the night.

Philadelphia has a rich history. William Penn founded the city in 1682 and named it. The Liberty Bell is housed there and so is Independence Hall, where the Declaration of Independence and the US Constitution were signed. Philadelphia had the second largest Black population in the nation in 1937, the year before Hattie Mae arrives. According to Richard Robert Wright Sr.—an educator and president of Citizens and Southern Bank and Trust Company— there was never a time when Black people were not in Philadelphia.

In *Once in a Blue Moon*, the precursor to *Hattie Mae Begins Again*, Hattie decides to take Cousin Abigail up on her offer and attend a private girls' school in Philadelphia. Once she arrives, she finds people like herself who have made their way north, as well as a thriving community that for generations has contributed to the betterment of the city while also facing its own particular challenges.

There are protests in the city and girls who are protesting against Hattie and her Southern roots, as classism shows up in Hattie's young life. There is one girl Hattie *can* depend on, though: Bert. I named her after my mother, Roberta. A few years back, I discovered Mom's 1945 high school yearbook. I learned that as a teen, she collected pictures of movie stars. Bert does too. She also wants to be a famous actress. I am not sure if my mother ever fancied herself on the big screen. But I created Bert as a tribute to her, the best mom in the world.

Early on in my research process, I took a walking tour of Philadelphia's Seventh Ward, where most African Americans resided during the time of my novel. One of the first places I went to was Mother Bethel, the first African Methodist Episcopal (A.M.E.) Church in America. Richard Allen, formerly enslaved, a minister and educator, was the founder. Because of its cultural and historical significance, Mother Bethel plays a notable role in my novel.

All my life I had heard about Cheyney University, just outside of Philadelphia. Only during the tour did I learn Cheyney started out as the Institute for Colored Youth right there in South Philly.

I took pictures outside Engine 11, an all-Black company of firefighters for many years. A pictorial tribute painted on the side of the current fire station includes Negro firefighters, men and women strolling along in beautiful clothing from a certain era, and W. E. B. Du Bois standing ten feet tall, it seems. His groundbreaking study on the people from the Seventh Ward is still being studied today.

Marian Anderson grew up in my city. Dr. Nathan Francis Mossell, a noted surgeon and founder of Frederick Douglass Memorial Hospital, made his mark there also. Robert Bogle, a restaurateur, became the first person to start catering as a profession. Pepper Pot Stew originated in Philly. Marion Turner Stubbs Thomas founded Jack and Jill, now a global organization for mothers and children.

Women and men, too many to name, made their homes and dreamed of new futures in Philadelphia. They established banks (three in the city at the time) and funeral homes; ran for political office and won; bought property; became landlords, entrepreneurs, maids, doctors, sea merchants, and more. But all was not smooth and easy. There was inadequate housing and shortages, discrimination, schools that left too many behind, along with a community always ready to stand up for itself.

Much of my story takes place on six blocks of Christian Street, often referred to as Black Doctors Row. During my research, I happily stumbled upon a document online that was a game changer. Commissioned by the Preservation Alliance of Greater Philadelphia, the report (Christian Street/Black Doctors Row Historic District Nomination) spelled out why Doctors Row should be registered as an historic district. This document gave me a deep dive into the block Hattie was to live. I now knew the names of current or past residents in each home, if they owned or rented. Thus, I learned each resident's occupation, the number of families or individuals living in the house and for how long, the character and design of the exterior of the home, who their neighbors were. Christian Street had as much personality as the people living there. To give homage, a few real-life individuals and businesses show up as neighbors or influential people in my book.

Librarians and aides assisted me often at The Free Library of Philadelphia, where I plowed through *The Philadelphia Tribune* conducting research. During my growing-up years, *The Tribune* was a staple in our household and thousands of others across Philadelphia. *The Tribune* gave us a bird's-eye view into a community that was passionate and purposeful about family, service, faith, education, political action, and standing proud and tall. This seemed even more true as I conducted my research.

Months into my research, I found my way to Temple University, where I took full advantage of the Charles L. Blockson Afro-American Collection. I arrived to dozens of books, papers, and photographs that had been curated and waiting for me. I read through rare papers, went through study after study as well as stats and sociological reports. Dr. Diane Turner, curator, and Aslaku Berhanu, librarian, were invaluable to my research.

On another visit, I made it to the University of Pennsylvania's Penn Libraries, Kislak Center for Special Collections, Rare Books and Manuscripts. Its library is beautiful, quiet as dawn in the woods. Staff wheeled in stacks of bound documents and left me to go through them. For the first time, I learned of Douglass Hospital, a mainstay in Philadelphia for decades. I sat in awe reading about the life and legacy of Marian Anderson, also a daughter of Philadelphia, and others who contributed to the city in big and small ways.

Living in the city, I had tons of photos on my phone and notes galore. My research journey was ending. But it was only the beginning of things for me as the author.

SHARON G. FLAKE

LIST OF SOURCES

PUBLICATIONS

Costantino, Maria. *Fashions of a Decade: The 1930s.* Facts on File, 1992.
Grafton, Carol Belanger, ed. *Fashions of the Thirties.* Dover Publications, Inc., 2006.
Lane, Roger. *William Dorsey's Philadelphia & Ours.* Oxford University Press, 1991.
Peacock, John. *The 1930s.* Fashion Sourcebooks. Thames and Hudson, 1997.
The Philadelphia Tribune. July 1938 through April 1939.
Wilkerson, Isabel. *The Warmth of Other Suns: The Epic Story of America's Great Migration.* Random House, 2011.

ARTICLES

"Back to the Farm." *The Philadelphia Tribune,* April 27, 1939.
"Tag Day Over the Top—$1,354." *The Philadelphia Tribune,* April 20, 1939.
"Deny Threat Nurses' Walkout at Hospital Admit Deficit at Douglass Over $6,000." *The Philadelphia Tribune,* August 24, 1939.

"The Negroes of Philadelphia Expert Study of Their Origins, Numbers, Character, Occupations and Social Life by RR Wright, Jr." *Public Ledger,* April 12, 1907.
"The Philadelphia Negro." *Public Ledger.*

ORGANIZATIONS

Penn Libraries: University of Pennsylvania's Kislak Center for Special Collections, Rare Books and Manuscripts
Temple University's Charles L. Blockson Afro-American Collection
Preservation Alliance of Greater Philadelphia
Philadelphia Register of Historic Places
Philadelphia Historical Commission: Christian Street/Black Doctors Row

ACKNOWLEDGMENTS

My deepest thanks to the people and organizations that helped to make this book possible: the Carnegie Library of Pittsburgh, Charles L. Blockson Afro-American Collection, the Free Library of Philadelphia, *The Philadelphia Tribune*, Preservation Alliance for Greater Philadelphia, and the University of Pennsylvania's Penn Libraries Kislak Center for Special Collections, Rare Books and Manuscripts.

Hugs and thanks to my editor, Gianna Lakenauth. You are incredible, perfect for me. Here's to more books.

Thank you to the entire Random House division and to everyone who has had a hand in making this book and getting it to readers.